# MESSIAH ONLINE

### CYBERPUNK UPLOADS - BOOK TWO

## SETH RAIN

Published by Human Fiction

ISBN: 978-1-9162775-6-4

Editing: Jane Hammett

Cover Design: Books Covered

# YOUR FREE NOVELLA IS WAITING!

Visit **sethrain.com** to download your free digital copy of the prequel novella: *The Rogue Watcher* and sign up to Seth's Reading Group emails.

# A BRIEF NOTE

I use British English spelling throughout this series. Not only am I a Brit, but this story is set in a futuristic London (or as you will discover: Lundun), and so it seems only right to use British English spelling. I hope this does not detract from your enjoyment.

Seth.

"I swear to God, in this light and on this evening,
London's become, the most beautiful thing I've seen."

**Editors - from the song: 'In This Light and on This Evening'**

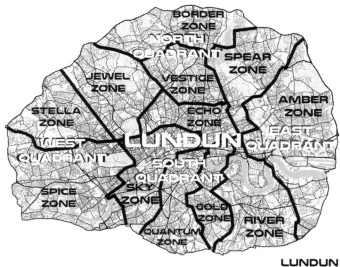

BORDER
ZONE
NORTH
QUADRANT
SPEAR
ZONE
JEWEL
ZONE
VESTIGE
ZONE
AMBER
ZONE
STELLA
ZONE
ECHO
ZONE
LUNDUN
EAST
QUADRANT
WEST
QUADRANT
SOUTH
QUADRANT
SPICE
ZONE
SKY
ZONE
GOLD
ZONE
RIVER
ZONE
QUANTUM
ZONE

LUNDUN
FR.E.DOM - 2112

# ONE

THE SPECTRUM DID what it had always done: dismantled light, time, and other worlds. And Blake did what he had always done: tried to keep up.

He rested the pulse cannon on his shoulder, wrapped his arm around it, and held a finger close to the trigger. One eye closed, he looked through the sight at the space shuttle, a kilometre away, poised on the launch pad, ready to break through the slab of grey sky.

In dark orange, Blake saw himself firing the cannon and striking the space shuttle, destroying it and the launch pad, along with the Fr.e.dom soldiers and drones that patrolled the area.

'Do you see it?' Angelus asked, on his knees behind him, looking over his shoulder. 'The spectrum?'

Blake ignored him and focused again on the space shuttle. But Angelus had broken his concentration. Blake was suddenly aware of the trees and the undergrowth all around him. Everything was damp from the last downpour of rain. He was unaccustomed to the smell of vegetation – sweet and earthy at the same time. The rain had stopped. In the dim light, the greens and browns surrounding him were vivid, as if he was once again in the spectrum.

Fr.e.dom's space programme was in the north-east of Border Zone, close to the wall. It was pointless trying to hide it. Each time they launched a space shuttle, the whole of Lundun shook.

'Do you see the spectrum?' Angelus asked again. 'Can we attack?'

Blake took the cannon from his shoulder and laid it on the ground. To his left and right were twenty androids, all willing to fight for the cause – for the revolution.

He met the eyes of two male androids, who stared back at him. Their expressions made him doubt yet again what they were doing. Blake was prepared to take risks with his own safety. But now, the decisions he and Angelus made had repercussions for others. He didn't even know their names. One of them wore a cap with a Speedball logo on it. Blake wanted to ask why he was there – why he was risking his life. Blake knew why *he* was doing it. But what about him? There was a tenderness in the android's eyes that over-whelmed him. Blake wanted to turn and run. If anything happened to the others, it would be because of him.

Angelus stooped in front of Blake and rested his hands on Blake's shoulders, making eye contact. 'Hey,' he said. 'Look at me.'

Blake inhaled deeply and stared into Angelus's eyes.

'This space shuttle,' Angelus said, 'is going to release a satellite that will stay above our heads, telling Fr.e.dom where we are, what we're doing, and who we're doing it with, 24/7. We can't let them do this. We have to stop Cardinal and Fr.e.dom right now.'

Blake had never understood how Angelus could be so sure about everything. Decisions seemed so straightforward for him. Such decision-making had never been easy for Blake.

'I see a world in which we destroy the space shuttle,' Blake said.

Angelus let go of Blake's shoulders and sighed with relief. 'That's good.'

'But I can't see what happens afterwards. I don't see what happens to us ... or to them.' Blake looked left and right at the androids, ready and waiting.

Angelus shook his head. 'We have to take this chance. We can't let them send this satellite into space. There'll be nowhere to hide. We have to do whatever it takes.'

'Won't Cardinal send another to replace it if we stop this one?'

'Eventually. But we need more time to convince androids in Lundun to fight with us. Before it's too late.'

The androids with him were ready to die for the cause. The manifesto had worked: it had attracted hundreds of androids who wanted the same thing: to fight back and to be free.

'There's a Fr.e.dom division on the other side of the hill.' Angelus pointed to the far right. 'They won't be expecting a full-on assault on the shuttle. But it won't take long before they're on to us. If we're quick – in and out – we can do this.'

Angelus checked his pistols were loaded before reaching across for the pulse cannon. Blake knew how powerful these cannons were – he'd used one to blow a hole in the north wall.

'We have to get closer,' Angelus said.

'You said we had to keep our distance.'

'We will.' Angelus lifted his head to peer through the undergrowth. 'Just a little further.'

'If their drones see us, we won't stand a chance.'

Blake glanced behind at the rows of bikes, ready and waiting for their getaway. He motioned for the androids on either side of him to take their positions. The sooner they did this, the sooner they could get out of there.

'Go,' he told Angelus. 'I'm behind you.'

Angelus, the cannon resting on his shoulder, crouched as he ran towards the trees ahead, then hid behind one. Blake arrived beside him and squinted around the tree. They were close enough to see a white mist spilling from the bottom of the space shuttle.

'Give it to me,' Blake said.

He took the cannon, knelt in the damp earth, took a deep breath and positioned the cannon on his shoulder. In the spectrum, he was the one who fired on the space shuttle.

The shuttle powered up, bursts of flames erupting from its rockets. Vibrations rumbled through the ground. Behind the shuttle, in the distance, a flock of birds swept from right to left. The space shuttle appeared to shrug off the callipers that held it still, fastening it to the scaffolding.

Blake hesitated. He hadn't seen what happened after he'd destroyed the space shuttle. Something told him it wasn't good.

'Do it,' Angelus said. 'Before it's too late.'

Blake's trigger finger twitched. He didn't want to do it.

'There'll be nowhere to hide,' Angelus said. 'Once that thing is in space, it's only a matter of time before Cardinal and Fr.e.dom regain total control of Lundun.'

Blake adjusted the cannon and peered through the sight. The world he'd seen in the spectrum materialised. The familiar colours, sounds and sensations he'd seen in his vision synced with reality.

His finger moved over the trigger. He pressed it.

The cannon made a whistling sound, then fired a pulse

of energy towards the shuttle. An orange sphere of heat bloomed on the surface of the space shuttle, which tipped to one side then exploded in an enormous ball of flame. The deafening boom made them duck for cover.

The plans they'd made before the attack meant nothing after the explosion. They, and the other androids, ran in all directions.

Already, drones were heading towards them.

Shouts of anger, pain and confusion disoriented Blake. He whirled around. The rattle of gunfire filled the air, bullets sending drones spinning off into trees and the undergrowth. Blake checked behind for Angelus, who was running, covering his head with his arms, dodging bullets from two drones that had arrived from different directions.

Loud voices echoed behind them, where they'd hidden the bikes.

'Go!' Blake shouted to the other androids. 'Get to your bikes!'

The drones shot two androids to the right of their group. They cried out in pain as they fell. The space shuttle had been more heavily protected than Blake had thought it would be. And the look Angelus gave him told Blake he thought the same.

Drones had pinned down the androids to his far left, trapped behind the Fr.e.dom division of soldiers.

Blake counted six other androids, not including himself and Angelus, who had reached the bikes but who were under fire.

'We can't go without them,' Blake shouted to Angelus. He spun his bike around, aimed it at the androids the drones had pinned down, and set off. As the surviving androids escaped on their bikes, he and Angelus rode towards another group, trapped between Fr.e.dom soldiers and drones.

Weaving through the trees, deep-blue solar-jets powering their bikes, Blake saw two androids dead on the ground. Angelus opened fire on two Fr.e.dom soldiers, reached an android, and helped him climb onto his bike. Blake found another and helped him onto his.

'Go, go!' the android shouted, slapping Blake's shoulder.

There were no other survivors in sight. Blake headed for Amber Zone to the south, Angelus close behind. A drone fired on them, but the android on the back of Angelus's bike shot it down, then they were clear. Blake found an open road and flashed through the border tolls, unmanned since the revolution had begun. Head down, squeezing the throttle to its maximum, Blake hurtled through Amber Zone to the furthest point east they could go before they hit the wall. He was the first to reach the meeting point. There, he powered down the bike and waited for the others to arrive.

'Thank you,' the android behind him said, climbing off.

Blake nodded, and they bumped fists.

Angelus arrived, followed by two more bikes.

'You said it would be a simple hit and run,' Blake said to Angelus.

'There was more of a presence than I'd expected.'

'No kidding!' Blake needed to keep his cool. Arguing with Angelus now would do no good. He watched as two more bikes appeared. One android fell off his bike, cradling his damaged arm.

Blake watched for signs of drones but, as the last of the bikes arrived, making nine survivors, there were none. He guessed they were safe for the time being.

Angelus was quiet. Blake could see he regretted taking

down the shuttle as much as he did. For all they knew, Fr.e.dom would have a replacement ready, making their attempt to stop it pointless.

The android Blake had seen before the attack sat on the ground holding a scorched baseball cap. The android lifted his head and met Blake's eyes before turning away. If Blake hadn't been sure that attacking the space shuttle had been a mistake, he was when he saw the android's blank, cold expression.

# TWO

BLAKE SPENT most of the night riding through the streets of Lundun. He couldn't shake the idea that he was responsible for the deaths of each android who had attacked the space shuttle with him. At the time, he knew it was a mistake, yet he'd listened to Angelus. He hated having to make those decisions. He was placing androids in danger, getting them killed.

The next morning, he sat on a balcony in an empty apartment they'd found in Amber Zone, looking over the border into River Zone. The city was still at this time of day, but there was a heavy restlessness in the air. Lundun was a different place now – made even more dangerous because of what he and Angelus had done the day before. There would be repercussions. Cardinal wouldn't let their act of treason go unpunished.

They still didn't know where Cardinal was keeping Lola, and with each day that passed, Blake felt there was less chance he'd ever see her again. Cardinal had taken her a month ago, and Blake had received the copy of *Songs of Innocence and Expe-*

*rience* with the note inside: *We can help one another unshackle those mind-forged manacles. I can help you. Don't give up – I'll be in touch when the time is right.* Angelus had tried to convince him that the Messiah had sent them the book and note, but Blake wasn't sure. They'd heard nothing from him since.

There was movement in the apartment.

'Don't blame yourself,' Angelus said, arriving beside him on the balcony.

In the distance, two drone-shuttles scudded across the horizon before turning away, revealing bright red tail-lights, then disappearing behind the towers of River Zone.

Blake told himself he should have been stronger. Even though he hadn't seen it in the spectrum, he knew that blowing up the space shuttle would endanger the androids who had followed them.

'I shouldn't have fired the cannon,' he said.

Angelus pointed up at the sky. 'But we couldn't let Cardinal get the satellite into orbit. There's no telling what he'd have done with that kind of control. Think of the androids we've saved by stopping the space shuttle.'

'But for how long? He'll use another space shuttle, construct another satellite.'

'Then we'll stop him again.' Angelus gripped the balcony rail. 'And then again if we have to.'

'It won't be so easy.'

Angelus didn't respond, just stared out across Lundun.

'You don't seem to care,' Blake said.

Angelus spun around. 'Care?'

'Androids died yesterday. Because of us.'

'They died for the cause – for the revolution. This isn't a game. We're trying to stop Cardinal and Fr.e.dom from taking control of this city, maybe even the world. Do you see

Cardinal releasing the hold he has on androids and humans once he has total power?'

Blake bowed his head.

'I don't,' Angelus said. 'It's now or never. We can't wait. Once Cardinal has the control he craves there'll be no way of fighting him.'

Blake was about to argue when his tracker buzzed against his wrist, notifying him the attack group in Quantum Zone, SQ, had breached the wall again. It was only a matter of time before Fr.e.dom sent in soldiers to take back Lundun. But if they could show the androids in Lundun what was possible, they might fight for the revolution when they were needed.

The digi-screen in the apartment flickered into life.

'Now there's a sight for sore eyes,' Angelus said, walking into the apartment.

Blake followed. On the digi-screen, Cardinal took his position behind a desk. He was dressed in white, his long blond hair groomed, his hands placed face-down on the table.

'Lundun is in a state of turmoil,' Cardinal said. 'But Fr.e.dom will return order and safety to our city. In time, Lundun will return to the wonderful city it has been for many years. This is our home, our android home, one that we all love and care for.' He took a moment, inhaling deeply. 'We are aware of the manifesto shared by a terrorist group intent on causing more disruption and more pain for Lundun's innocent, law-abiding residents. I want to assure you that we will eliminate this group, along with any other small uprisings within the city.'

Angelus sighed noisily.

'One of the crowning glories of android life has been the development of the Net,' Cardinal went on. 'It truly is a marvel of our civilisation.' Cardinal moved in his chair, his expression changing from sympathetic to stern. 'But it is time for androids themselves to contribute to the wellbeing of their home, their mother city. If the fighting and turmoil do not cease, then we will have no choice but to take down the Net.'

'He's desperate,' Angelus said.

'Over ninety-five per cent of androids in Lundun visit the Net each day,' Cardinal continued. 'But, I repeat, unless the fighting and disruption end, Fr.e.dom will have no choice but to take down the Net.'

Cardinal stood. The camera pulled back to take in his height. He swept a hand through his hair. 'This is your last chance, Lundun. Take control of your neighbourhoods and ensure peace is maintained.'

The screen faded to black, replaced with a recorded Speedball game.

'Can he do that?' Blake asked Angelus.

'I'm not sure. Maybe, if he destroys the servers.'

'Where are they?'

Angelus shrugged. 'I'm not sure anyone outside Fr.e.dom knows.'

Blake thought about what Cardinal had said. 'Why would he do that? What would he gain from destroying the Net?'

'I guess androids who spend their time online don't provide anything worthwhile for the city.'

'But what about all the people who have uploaded permanently? If Cardinal destroys the servers and the Net, won't they be lost forever?'

'I guess so,' Angelus said. 'But uploading is illegal. Cardinal will say they only have themselves to blame.'

'He's punishing them.'

'So what do we do? Call off the fighting?'

Blake stroked his chin. 'That's what Cardinal wants.'

'Five million androids have uploaded permanently.'

'Would Cardinal really do it?' Blake asked.

Angelus folded his arms. 'I don't know.' He shook his head. 'No, I do know. He'll do it.'

Blake's tracker buzzed with messages from the other revolution groups dotted around Lundun. 'They want to know what to do.'

Angelus stared at Blake, waiting for him to decide.

'I don't see the spectrum,' Blake said. 'If that's what you're waiting for.'

'No,' Angelus said. 'I didn't think so. But we need to decide.'

'You mean *I* need to decide?'

Angelus offered a gentle head tilt and sympathetic smile.

With all tough decisions, Blake thought, the moment you settled on one side, the other seemed more attractive. So many androids had died already. If they gave in now, all their lives would have been lost ... for nothing. But, if they continued, many more lives would be lost, including possibly all five million androids who had uploaded to the Net.

His tracker buzzed with more messages, more questions from the androids fighting on their side.

'Blake?' Angelus asked.

Blake closed his eyes and waited. They had come so far. To go back now? He couldn't live with himself if he did that. 'We can't give in. We have to keep going.'

Angelus nodded. Blake watched for clues in his face to reassure him it was the right choice. He didn't see any.

# THREE

THE LIFT in the apartment tower Blake and Angelus were hiding in was broken. Blake hated having to keep moving, but until they'd come up with a plan, there was no other way. He led the way up the stairs. On the first floor, they heard shouts coming from the apartments to the left of the stairwell. Blake pushed through the door and ran along the corridor. A woman covering her mouth, tears streaming down her face, met him. She saw Blake and pointed through an open door.

'In there. He did it. He did it!'

Blake and Angelus ran into the apartment.

'He said he'd wait for me,' the woman said through sobs.

On the bed was an android hooked up to a terminal, his body still. Blake's shoulders fell. He'd seen it before. Androids who had uploaded.

'He said he'd wait for me,' the woman said again. 'We only had enough Sky-blue for one, and he said he'd wait until we had enough for both of us.' She cried out again, then ran to the bed and began thumping the man's chest.

Angelus grabbed her from behind and picked her up, her arms and legs still swinging.

The terminal beside the android's bed was off. The upload was complete.

'If you destroy his body,' Angelus said, 'he won't be able to download back.'

'He's not coming back!' she shouted. 'He's never coming back. He's left me here, in this hell, alone!'

Blake felt her pain. He wanted to help her, but didn't know what to say or do.

Finally, the woman went limp. Angelus let her go. She fell onto the bed, her arms outstretched, reaching for the android and hugging him, crying into his chest.

Angelus gave Blake a sympathetic look, then shrugged. He knew, as well as Blake did, there was no way the android was going to download again. It was possible, but very few androids did it. Blake didn't know any who had.

Blake and Angelus waited.

Eventually she slid from the mattress and sat with her back against the frame of the bed, her head low.

Blake sat down beside her.

She turned to him. He couldn't remember seeing a sadder face.

'It should have been both of us.'

'But it's not safe,' he said. 'Uploading is illegal. We don't know what Fr.e.dom will do to those who upload.'

She shook her head. 'The Messiah will protect us.'

Already, Blake's sympathy was waning. 'Don't believe everything you hear.'

'I do believe it. I have to.' She pointed to the window. 'I can't stay here.'

Blake followed her line of sight. 'I know. But we can make this place better. It doesn't have to be like this.'

The woman laughed sarcastically. 'This place is not for us. It's not for androids. It hurts too much. We're trapped here. The only place I feel alive is the Net. But I can barely afford an hour a day. The rest of the time, I'm working, doing everything I can to find money to go back there.'

Blake had tried to understand. But whenever he talked to androids addicted to the Net, he saw them as weak – in denial.

'But your life doesn't have to be like that. Don't you see? We're fighting back. We're fighting Fr.e.dom.'

She shrugged half-heartedly. 'It won't do any good.' She looked up at the android on the bed. 'The only way out of this hell is to upload. To be with the Messiah. He will save us.'

Angelus sighed, then helped the woman stand. 'What's your name?'

'Kaz. It cost everything we had to buy that Sky-blue Mirth. We were saving for another dose. But he's left me here. Alone.'

An arm around her shoulders, Angelus guided her to a chair beside a table and helped her sit.

Kaz held her head in her hands for a while, sobbing, then took her hands away and smiled through her tears. 'We saw it.'

Angelus looked at Blake, confused.

'What did you see?' Blake asked.

'The world he has built for us. We saw it. We even picked out a home. We were going to live beside a lake. At the far end of the lake was a cliff, and in the middle of the cliff was a waterfall. There's nothing like this place.' She pointed again at the window. 'I can't stay here. I can't stay in Lundun. In this apartment, in this reality.'

15

Blake couldn't take his eyes off her. She radiated a combination of sadness and hope.

'Can you help me?' she asked eagerly. 'Can you get me the Sky-blue?'

Blake shook his head. 'I'm sorry.'

Maybe he could get it for her. If he tried. But it wouldn't have been right. When Cardinal destroyed the Net, he would kill all the androids who had uploaded. He couldn't be responsible for that.

Angelus apologised too. She wiped her eyes and sniffed. 'It's not your fault.' She twisted a copper ring on her finger. 'Have you ever seen a waterfall?'

The question surprised Blake, and he wasn't sure how to respond.

'Have you?' she asked him again.

'No. I've not seen a waterfall.'

'I have. I remember the way the light hit the water – it rose in a haze of spray, the light refracting through it, creating a rainbow. It was beautiful.'

Blake held his breath, imagining the sight. It reminded him of the spectrum.

'The falling water was so loud. You've no idea how loud a waterfall is. And the smell ... so clean, new, fresh.' She wiped her eyes again. 'And now I'll never have the chance to see it again. I'm stuck here.'

'There are waterfalls here,' Blake said. 'On Earth.'

With a quick, disgusted snort, she threw her hands in the air. Blake regretted saying it.

'We're trapped here,' she said. 'What good are waterfalls on Earth when we're all trapped?'

'Not for much longer,' Blake said. Angelus raised an eyebrow. But Blake really believed it.

'You won't stop them,' Kaz said. 'Fr.e.dom will be back. You'll see.'

'We're going to fight them,' Blake said.

'It's no good.' Kaz stared at the android on the bed. 'That was my only chance. I won't get that Sky-blue Mirth on my own. I'm stuck here. I should have taken it before he did. But I couldn't do that to him. Does that make me a fool?'

Blake wanted to leave. There was nothing he could do to help her. She'd already given up. He stood.

'Is there anything we can do?' Angelus asked her.

She shook her head, staring at the android on the bed.

'I'll check on you later,' Angelus said. 'If that's okay?'

She didn't respond.

Blake left the room, followed by Angelus. They reached the stairwell and continued the climb to their temporary apartment. He was hearing more and more often about this Messiah, and he didn't like what he'd heard.

# FOUR

THEY SPENT some time in the apartment in River Zone, working out which part of the wall they should attack next. It didn't seem to matter which part of the wall they went to; there were more Fr.e.dom soldiers arriving all the time. It was strange, and he didn't know if it said more about him than the situation, but the longer this went on, and the more androids who joined them, the less reasonable it was to think they might succeed. But there was no turning back.

Blake stared at the map of Lundun spread out on the table between them.

'I've been thinking,' Angelus said, sitting back in his chair. 'We need to get word to the androids inside the Net. We need to get them out of there in case Cardinal carries out his threat.'

'How do we do that?'

'We go straight to the android who's leading them. The Messiah.'

'You have to let it go. He's just a hacker – a crook. That's if he even exists. The whole thing is a fantasy androids have made up.'

'He's the one who sent that note. I know he is.'

Blake rolled his eyes. 'Not that again.'

'I know you don't believe what people say about him. But there has to be something in it. What if he's helping androids?'

'We've seen the bodies of the androids who have uploaded,' Blake said, annoyed. 'All stretched out and cold. What he's doing is wrong. Uploading is suicide. And this coder they're all calling the Messiah is helping androids do it.'

'But what if it's real and he's offering them a better world?'

Blake hesitated. He'd thought about it many times, but he always came back to the notion that living in Lundun, on Earth, was real, and that uploading to the Net was unreal – a fantasy. There was no value in living a fantasy, a lie.

'He has a huge following,' Angelus said. 'More and more people are uploading all the time because of him.'

'It's a scam. I wouldn't be surprised if Cardinal was behind it somehow. All that digital eternity bullshit...'

Angelus pointed upwards. 'Is it any surprise that androids want to believe what the Messiah tells them? What do most of them have to live for? It's better to live in a digital world. Permanently.'

'When Cardinal destroys the servers and the Net goes down, they'll be lost forever. What the Messiah is doing is dangerous. He can't give them what they want. He's making empty promises.'

'They want to believe in something,' Angelus said. 'In someone. He gives them that.'

'Do *you* believe what he says? That uploading is an escape? That he can give them an eternity inside the Net?'

'No, of course not. All I'm saying is, I can see why androids are following him.'

It made Blake angry to hear Angelus talk about the Messiah.

Angelus shifted uncomfortably in his chair. 'You're not going to like it. But I think we have to go into the Net and find him.'

'Hell, no!'

'Hear me out.'

Blake waited for Angelus to continue, already thinking of reasons to refuse.

'We can tell him what's happening, say we need his help. He can tell his followers to unplug – download back into their bodies. It won't be forever, just until Cardinal takes back his threat.'

'And you think he'd do that?' Blake scoffed. 'Just because we ask him to?'

'We have to try. And what if the note *was* from him? He said he can help us. He was talking about Lola – I know he was. He can help us find her.'

'How do you know he was talking about Lola?'

'It has to be that.'

Blake was deep in thought. He considered calling on the spectrum, but this was too abstract, too stretched out in time. 'The note wasn't from him.'

'You don't know that. He's a powerful android. I know he'll help us find Lola and help save the androids who have uploaded.' Angelus nodded to himself.

There was something on his mind, Blake could tell.

'What is it?' Blake asked. 'What's wrong?'

'It's ... I have some news on Lola.'

Blake's stomach sank. He couldn't speak, scared Angelus was going to tell him she was dead.

'I know someone who might know where she is. We're old friends and I know she's had many androids at her house. Important androids. Androids who deal with Fr.e.dom.'

'Why didn't you tell me before?'

'I'm not sure she'll be able to help us. Or if her helping might get her into trouble. But we're running out of options.'

'Take me there,' Blake said.

Angelus paused.

'Now,' Blake said, and walked out of the apartment.

They set off north into Amber Zone, where Fr.e.dom recruited most of its soldiers. The streets were empty. Since the revolution had begun, recruitment to Fr.e.dom's cause had accelerated. It was tough for androids from Amber Zone to refuse the regular meals and regular pay of a soldier. EQ had been the most impoverished quadrant for so long. One by one, the androids who lived there joined Fr.e.-dom's military divisions. Blake hated the idea that androids ignored the authoritarian control Fr.e.dom had over the androids in Lundun. If they simply refused – all the androids at once – he was sure Fr.e.dom wouldn't be able to stop them.

Angelus pulled his bike onto a long drive that led them through an archway of steel, covered in blue lights. At the end of the driveway was a brightly lit turntable, upon which were three bikes equipped with the latest red solar-jets – state-of-the-art. They pulled up on the turntable and waited. Angelus scanned all around. The ground began to vibrate. The turntable started to revolve, descending at the same time.

'Don't worry,' Angelus said. 'It's supposed to do this.' He looked all around as they sank further below ground. 'I think.'

Finally, the sides of the walls glowed yellow with the lights from beneath the turntable. A large room appeared, decorated in shades of light blue and pale yellows. A tall woman with long red hair, dressed in a long black dress, one hand holding a full champagne glass, walked towards them. She stood with a hand on her hip, a leg outstretched, her dress parted either side of it.

'Angelus,' she said when the motor beneath the turntable finally cut out. 'You look tired.'

'You look amazing,' Angelus said. 'As always.'

'I'm having an end-of-the-world party,' she said with a wry smile.

Angelus walked over to her. 'No better time for a party, I guess.'

'No need to tidy up the day after.' She air-kissed Angelus on both cheeks before glancing at Blake. 'Who's your handsome friend?'

She was a beautiful woman, and she knew it.

'This is Francesca,' Angelus said to Blake.

'Blake.' He offered his hand.

She ignored his hand and puckered her lips invitingly. He did as she wanted. She smelled as good as she looked.

'That's an unusual name,' she said. 'I like it.'

'We need your help,' Angelus said.

'My help? With your friend? Lola?'

'Yes,' Blake said.

Both Francesca and Angelus glanced at him, clearly surprised at his eagerness.

'I see,' Francesca said, smiling at Blake. 'She's your girl?'

'No,' Blake said. 'It's not like that.'

She raised an eyebrow. 'Sure, handsome. It's never like that.'

Heat rushed to his face. He wondered what kind of

programming led to androids blushing. It made no sense. And yet, it was just another idiosyncrasy that proved androids were created to be like humans. It was these small details that on the surface appeared irrelevant, that resulted in an android capturing the essence and appearance of a human.

'Do you know where she is?' Angelus asked.

'You know I don't like to tell tales on my guests, Angelus.' She smiled coyly. 'But for you, I can divulge a little.'

Angelus said nothing.

It was clear to Blake that the two of them had history. He watched as they circled one another.

Francesca ran a hand through her long red hair and swept it behind her shoulders. 'Cardinal, it seems, is fascinated with your friend.' For a brief moment, she appeared disgusted. 'I've known several human women in my time, and I'd say she is the most ordinary-looking of all of them.'

She glanced at Blake, perhaps to measure his reaction. He tried not to give anything away.

'I can see why some androids might see her as pretty,' she said. 'I'll say that much. Cardinal is certainly smitten.'

She was saying this for Blake's benefit, so he made an effort not to bite. Then, he couldn't shake the thought of what Cardinal might be doing to Lola while he was wasting time.

Francesca sighed, looking more sympathetic. 'They've taken her shadow's body from the underground cavern in Vestige Zone – where she was killed.'

He remembered seeing her being shot by drones. She'd waited for it to happen, knowing the price she'd have to pay for killing Rex. 'Why?' he asked. 'What for?'

Francesca drank from her glass. 'Who knows exactly?

My guess: Cardinal wants to understand how her shadow – and their connection – works.'

'He has his own shadows,' Angelus said.

'Does he?' she asked, surprised. 'An android with their own shadow. Whatever next?'

The thought of Cardinal doing tests on Lola's shadow filled Blake with another wave of anger. What was Cardinal hoping to achieve?

'Do you know where they're keeping her?' Angelus asked.

'From what I've heard, I'd say she's still in Lundun. Most likely SQ. Sky Zone, maybe.'

Blake had been hoping for a more specific location. But it was a start.

'You won't get her back,' she said, her eyes on Blake, again testing him, seeing how far she could go before breaking him.

'What do you know about the Messiah?' Blake asked her.

She looked taken aback. She sipped her drink and composed herself. 'He's a wonderful man. Charismatic, charming, extremely clever.' She raised an eyebrow at Angelus. 'And, by all accounts, extremely handsome.'

Angelus stared at her, unmoved.

'He can help you,' she said more seriously. 'If you're prepared to follow him. He can help you find your friend, I'm sure. He dislikes Cardinal almost as much as you do.'

'I don't think that's possible,' Blake said.

She shrugged, her eyes on Angelus.

'So, how can we find him?' Blake asked.

'I'm afraid I can't help you with that. He's a bit of a Houdini. He tends to find you, rather than the other way around.'

Blake was already running out of patience with this guy and he'd not even met him.

'Thank you, Francesca,' Angelus said.

'Please.' She kissed him again. 'Frankie. Like old times.'

'Frankie,' he said.

'Surely you can stay for a drink,' she said to Angelus, her face close to his.

Angelus clearly didn't know what to say. Blake felt compelled to help him out before he said or did something stupid. 'We should go.'

'Very well,' she said to Angelus. 'Don't be a stranger.' She raised her hand and walked away.

Blake and Angelus watched her all the way to the stairs.

'You and her?' he asked Angelus.

'Me and her,' Angelus said, transfixed.

'She's something else.'

'You have no idea.'

# FIVE

ARCHER HAD HAILED BLAKE, asking to see him. Because
Archer had helped Blake spread the word about the manifesto using Fr.e.dom's media outlets, Blake was worried
something bad might have happened to him. They agreed
to meet in River Zone. Blake and Angelus waited for him on
Thames Barrier Bridge.

'We need to get on to the Net,' Angelus said. 'We're
wasting time.'

'This will be important,' Blake said. 'Archer never hails
me. Usually he shows up uninvited at the worst time.'

'We have to find the Messiah.'

Blake scrunched up his face. 'Do we have to call him
that?'

'What should we call him?'

'He must have an actual name. What is it?'

'I'm not sure anyone knows.'

'What about Dave? I bet he's called Dave, or Bob.'

'And you think the art dealer will get us close to him?'

Blake nodded. 'Bo told me he knows the Messiah. He
said they were friends. Even though they'd only met once.'

Ahead, across the bridge, Archer was walking towards them, trying to appear inconspicuous but failing.

'Arch,' Blake said.

Archer put a finger to his lips and jerked his head. They followed him down a set of stone steps and beneath the bridge. Beside them was the Thames Barrier, its huge silver domes towering over them.

'What's going on?' Blake asked.

'Come closer,' Archer said, beckoning them. 'I'm guessing you had something to do with the shuttle exploding and Cardinal threatening to destroy the Net?'

'I don't know what you mean,' Blake said, deadpan.

'Yes,' Angelus said, giving Blake a sharp nod, before again focusing on Archer. 'That was us.'

'You have to stop Cardinal from destroying the Net,' Archer said. 'There are millions of androids who have uploaded. If Cardinal destroys the servers, they'll be killed. All of them.'

'We know,' Blake said. 'But what can we do about it?'

'Either you do as Cardinal says and stop the fighting, or you get the data out of the servers somehow. Each android consciousness exists in those servers. If you can stop Cardinal from damaging the servers, great. If not, you need to get the data out of there before he kills them all.'

'But how do we do that?' Angelus asked. 'The amount of data we'd need to transfer would be huge. There's no way to do it.'

'The Messiah,' Archer said.

'Come on!' Blake said. 'How did I know you were going to say that? What is it with this guy?'

Archer spoke quietly. 'He can help us.'

'Not you too?' Blake said.

'Where are the servers?' Angelus asked.

'On the Isle of Wight. Underground. They work, but they're outdated. I've heard that Fr.e.dom wants to take down the Net and begin again. Cardinal knows about those who have uploaded permanently. He wants to destroy the Net with them inside.'

'So this has nothing to do with the revolution? He was going to do it anyway?'

'Maybe. I guess all this has made Cardinal accelerate his plans. Either way, you need to get the androids out of there.'

'And how can the Messiah help us do that?'

'He hates Fr.e.dom. He can help – I know he can.'

'How?' Angelus asked.

Archer shrugged. 'He's fighting against Fr.e.dom too. I don't know how exactly, but I know he will help us.'

'What about all the promises he's making?' Blake asked. 'Sending each consciousness to a digital eternity? He can't do that. Can he?'

'I don't know what he's planning to do,' Archer said.

'Whatever he does online,' Angelus said, 'surely there has to be something here in physical reality to store the data of his world and each consciousness inside it? Even if he uploads them all, there has to be actual servers to store all the data?'

Archer shifted uncomfortably. 'Look, I don't know how, and I don't know when, but I believe the Messiah is going to save them.'

'Why?' Blake asked. 'Why would you believe that?'

Archer paused. He took his time to breathe in and out deeply. 'I just do.'

'He could be a crackpot for all we know.'

'You have to try,' Archer said. 'Knowing where the servers are is useless if you don't have the ability to extract the data.'

'But if he believes he's taking them all to a digital heaven, or whatever he's spouting, won't he think what we want to do is pointless?'

'Maybe,' Archer said. 'You'll have to convince him, I guess.'

'How do we find him?'

Archer checked behind and then peered over Blake's shoulder. 'I don't know.'

'Great,' Blake said. 'What about Lola? Do you know where they're keeping her?'

Archer shook his head. 'Sorry.'

'We've been told she could be in Sky Zone,' Angelus said.

Archer gripped Blake's shoulder and squeezed. 'I'll keep my eyes and ears open.'

The river rushing beside Blake caught his attention. He always felt a sense of timelessness being beside the river – as though, at any moment, a sixteenth-century frigate might pass by, making its way to the docks. Sometimes it felt like the river came to the city, instead of the city being built beside the river. Maybe all huge civilisations were born beside water.

'Come with us,' Blake said to Archer. 'It's too dangerous. Fr.e.dom will know you helped with the manifesto. It's only a matter of time before they catch up with you.'

Archer shook his head. 'There's too much to do. I've started this with you. I want to see it through to the end. Being close to Fr.e.dom's media means I'm getting tiny bits of inside information all the time.'

'Be careful,' Blake said, lowering his gaze to meet Archer's.

'How will you get deep enough into the Net to reach the Messiah?' Archer asked. 'He'll be hidden well.'

'I know someone who can help,' Blake said. 'An art dealer in EQ.'

'Can he get you the right Mirth? It won't be the everyday stuff you need in order to reach him. The deeper you go into the Net, the stronger, more sophisticated Mirth you need.'

'I think so.'

'I hope so.' Archer checked both ways along the river before saying goodbye and heading up the steps.

'Are we going to see Bo?' Angelus asked Blake.

'He's the only android I know who will have the right Mirth and get us on the Net and close enough to the...'

'Messiah?' Angelus said.

Blake shook his head as he led the way up the steps. 'He'd better be something special after all this. To hear people talk about this guy, you'd think he walks on water.'

'I've heard he can. On the Net, at least.'

'Of course he can,' Blake said. 'What kind of Messiah would he be if he couldn't?'

# SIX

BLAKE HAD BEEN ONLINE several times – but never for long. He had to be careful. He knew how addictive the Net – and Mirth – could be. He'd seen it time and again. The Net beat the real world hands down, and androids soon went back for more. And more.

'Breathe in deeply,' Angelus said.

He sat opposite Angelus, his eyes closed, his legs crossed, his hands on his knees. They'd been meditating each day for weeks. Blake wasn't sure it was helping to control the spectrum, or the pain he experienced after the many worlds vanished again.

'We need to keep up the practice,' Angelus said.

'Is meditating really necessary right now, with all this going on?'

'You are a living proponent of the many worlds interpretation of quantum mechanics. An actual living, breathing gateway to other realities. So yes, it's necessary if you're going to learn to control it.'

'There's no need to get all technical on me.'

'I'm reminding you how amazing this is. You need to

learn to harness it. Describe to me again what it's like. Remember: mental focus.'

Blake took a deep breath. 'The world divides into a spectrum of waves from red to violet. Each one shows me a different possibility. I navigate these worlds to find the most beneficial one.'

'You're not doing it,' Angelus said. 'I can tell you're not focusing.'

'I am. I will...' Blake rotated his shoulders, shook his arms, closed his eyes and tried to clear his mind.

Angelus spoke quietly. 'If you train your mind, you'll be able to call on the spectrum at will.'

Blake inhaled, more slowly this time, held his breath, then concentrated on the air leaving his body.

'Good,' Angelus said. 'Better.'

Lola was out there somewhere. And the thing that really got to Blake was, she might be close by, right there in Lundun. She might only be a few hundred metres away for all he knew. There were so many places to hide someone in Lundun. He couldn't stop thinking about how she looked when she held Jack's dead body. She'd given Blake up to keep Jack alive, but Wan killed him anyway. In her eyes, Blake saw she'd given up. She went with Stig freely in the end, without putting up a fight. Maybe if he and Angelus found her, she wouldn't want to go with them, anyway. Who knew what Cardinal was doing to her? It hurt to think about, made him feel empty ... hollow.

'Focus,' Angelus said. 'Your mind is wandering. I can see it.'

Blake clenched his jaw and shut his eyes. He searched for the colours. Maybe if he concentrated hard enough, he'd see where Lola was. But his ability had never worked like that. It seemed to operate without him ... despite him. He opened his eyes.

Angelus stared back at him. 'You're restless. This won't work unless you give in to your subconscious mind. That's where the spectrum resides. I'm sure of it.'

'We have to find Lola,' Blake said.

Angelus sighed and his face softened. 'We will.'

'What do you think Cardinal is doing to her?'

Angelus stared at the ground. 'I don't know. But dwelling on it won't help her.'

He was right. But Blake couldn't help it. Dwelling on it was all he could do, or wanted to do.

'Can we try one more time?' Angelus asked. 'This time, let it all go.'

'I'll try.'

Again, Blake shook his arms and head and closed his eyes.

'Breathe in,' Angelus said. 'Slowly.'

Blake breathed in and out, focusing on each inhalation and exhalation. Listening to Angelus's voice helped him focus on the breath. Lola came to the forefront of his mind, but he let her go. Then Cardinal, then Mia, his dead wife, and then Lola again. Each time he told himself to let them go and to focus on the breath. Minutes passed.

In the distance, a deep red reverberated then unfolded like a flower opening. Beside it, a fan of orange light rippled by, shifting to a luminous yellow at the edges. It was the spectrum, opening up. In each world, Blake was sitting on the floor opposite Angelus. And in each one, he looked the same. But when he examined the worlds more closely, there were differences. Only slight, but they were there. His breathing might have been out of sync, or Angelus's eyelids might have flickered differently. In some, a fly hovered above Angelus's head. The light collapsed into one beam of white and Blake opened his eyes. Dizzy, he placed a hand on the ground beside him.

'I did it,' he said. 'I saw the spectrum.'

Angelus smiled. 'Good. I think that shows you can harness it.'

Blake held his head – there was a dull pain at the base of his skull. 'But the more I use it, and the deeper I go, the more it hurts when I come out of the trance.'

'We have to be careful,' Angelus said. 'I'm hoping you can train yourself to do this, making it easier each time.'

'If anything, it's getting harder.'

'We'll see what we can do about that.'

Blake stood. 'We need to see Bo.'

'Do you trust him?' Angelus asked.

'As much as I trust anyone, I guess.'

'We don't know who Cardinal has reached out to. He'll be watching us closely.'

'He has no control inside the Net,' Blake said, more as a question.

'I'm not so sure,' Angelus said. 'I think Cardinal knows more, and can do a lot more, than he's letting on.'

Blake loaded up the bike and got on. With Angelus riding his own bike, they rode north to River Zone. Bo was only interested in partying, his champagne, and his art collection. Blake wasn't sure he'd be willing to help them get onto the Net. But he was the only android he knew who might be able to help get them close to the Messiah.

It had stopped raining, and the early evening was still and balmy. Neon ads crawled up and down the towers of the city, selling things androids didn't need but desired anyway. The latent tension in the air made the city thrum with apprehension – and made Blake nervous. Lundun knew something. Lundun was older than everyone who lived there. It was a simple thing to think, yet it struck him as important. None of them knew what they were doing there – not really. They were all just trying to survive to see the next sunrise. And yet, if he listened closely enough, Lundun had a plan, Lundun had a purpose. It was hidden, but it was always there, a part of history so expansive it spoke a different language – the language of cities.

# SEVEN

IT TOOK them almost twenty minutes to convince the militia surrounding Bo's apartment tower to let them in.

Bo, dressed in a long pink dress, offered them champagne and apologised for the time it had taken to get inside. 'I can't be too careful these days, my dears.'

'It's nine in the morning,' Blake said, taking a glass.

Bo huffed and waved his hand. 'If you've never had a champagne breakfast, you've not lived.'

Blake glanced at Angelus, who shrugged and took a glass.

'That's the spirit,' Bo said, sitting on a settee, crossing his legs and throwing a pink scarf over his shoulder. 'To what do I owe the pleasure?' He sat forward quickly. 'It's my art, isn't it? You want to give it back.'

Blake still felt guilty about taking the paintings from Bo. 'Sorry. It's not that.'

Bo held up his hand. 'It's okay. I'm over them. I am, really.' He wiped a mock tear from beneath his right eye.

'I remember you said you'd met the...' Blake glanced at

Angelus, not wanting to use his name. 'The Messiah? You have one of his paintings.'

Bo closed his eyes and raised his chin. 'Oh good lord, do I know the Messiah? I'm in love with him, dear.' Bo placed a hand on his chest. 'Have you seen him?'

Blake downed his champagne. 'No. I don't think so.'

'You'd know if you had.'

'Can you arrange a meeting?' Angelus asked. 'We need to speak to him.'

Bo covered his mouth then, in a flurry of movement, stood, handing Blake his own glass of champagne. Blake finished that one too.

'What reason do you have for wanting to see the Messiah?' Bo's tone was different, as if he knew something important, a secret Blake needed to know.

'We're trying to find a friend,' Blake said.

'And we want him to warn those androids who have uploaded what Cardinal plans to do to the Net.'

Bo exaggerated a sad expression. 'It's a horrible thought. But it's their own fault. I've said time and again that the Net is for the weak, those not strong enough to face reality. They shouldn't do it. I love the Messiah, but I don't like this idea. Not one bit.'

'I don't blame them for uploading,' Angelus said, looking out of the window. 'They want to escape this place.'

'Don't say that,' Bo said. 'In order for beauty to exist in the world, we need the ugly. For love to mean anything, we need hate. For life to have value, we must be reminded of death every day. The Net ignores such things. In time, nothing will have any meaning for anyone who exists in that place. There will be no forward, backward, up or down.'

Blake had never heard anyone speak that way. He held his breath and recited the words over in his head. There was a truth to it but, at the same time, it was exhausting to consider it, never mind live through it.

'Can you help us?' Blake asked.

Bo walked over to his wall of art and sighed. 'I can help you,' he said. 'But I want my art back.'

It surprised Blake. Bo had spoken assuredly, like a businessman, totally out of character.

Angelus was staring at Blake, willing him to agree. But Blake had no idea how he was going to get Bo's artwork back from Stig. They had parted on terms that meant it was favourable to stay out of Stig's way. As long as Blake did that, there was a chance he could survive a while longer.

'I don't know if I can,' Blake said.

Angelus's shoulders dropped.

Bo stared at one of his paintings. 'Where there is a will, there is a way.'

'Is there nothing else we can do for you that would make you help us?' Blake asked.

'If I do this for you, there is a chance that the Messiah will have nothing more to do with me. If he thinks I've used our friendship for my own ends, he may refuse to see me again. And my dear, then I would be heartbroken. You're asking something considerable of me. So I must ask something considerable of you.'

'That's fair,' Angelus said. 'We will get the paintings.'

Blake gave Angelus a questioning stare.

Again, Bo's demeanour changed. He clapped his hands. 'I so want those paintings back on the wall. It was a mistake to sell them to you. I hope you don't mind me saying so. We're friends. We are, aren't we? We're dear friends now.'

'No problem,' Blake said.

'I will make the preparations here. I have everything you need to get onto the Net and meet with him.'

'We'll be back later tonight,' Angelus said.

Blake was already wondering how they might get the paintings back without losing their heads. He knew Angelus was thinking he could use the spectrum to get them. But just the thought of doing so hurt his head. The more he used it, the harder it was to recover. Now and then, he felt the pressure of what he'd done at the back of his head, in the base of his neck. Angelus dismissed the pain, but Blake suspected there would come a point when the spectrum would kill him. He didn't know how or why, but every time he saw the spectrum, he felt as though he was paying a price that eventually he would not be able to afford.

In a daze, Blake walked out of the apartment and into the lift. He wanted to rest, to stop a while, but it never stopped. Lundun never stopped. His head never stopped.

'How will we get the paintings back from Stig?' he asked Angelus.

'I don't know yet, but if it's the only way we can get close to the Messiah, we have to think of a way.'

'Stig isn't going to welcome us.'

'No, I guess not.'

'We have to give him something in return,' Blake said. 'He's a businessman.'

They stood in the lift, facing the closed doors, thinking hard.

The lift stopped, and the doors opened with a ding.

'You,' Angelus said, staring at Blake. 'We offer him you. You can make deliveries for him. He knows about your ability. He'll jump at the chance to work with you again.'

'I can't work for him,' Blake said. 'I can't.'

Angelus stepped out of the lift. 'Then you need to come up with something else, and quick.'

# EIGHT

BLAKE STOOD in front of Stig's apartment tower, taking in its full height. The top floors vanished into dense clouds.

'I can't believe we're doing this,' Blake said.

Angelus arrived next to him. 'Like you said. Stig's a businessman.'

'He sounded willing to listen to what we have to say.' Blake glanced at his wrist and the modified tracker, now freeing him to travel where he wanted. 'But I don't trust him.'

'What does your gut tell you?'

'It's telling me to run!'

'Too late for that now.' Angelus pointed at two of Stig's men walking towards them. One of them was Trevor.

'You're a tough one to kill,' Blake said to Trevor.

Trevor said nothing, simply stopped a metre away and waited for them to follow him into the apartment tower.

'I'm sorry about shooting you,' Angelus said to Trevor.

Trevor didn't budge. His eyes were fixed on Blake, who walked past him, sniffing at the stench coming off the big guy – a combination of deep-fried v-meat and Chilli-Grit, the newest flavour.

They walked into the apartment block. The doors of the 'God is android' lift were open, waiting. Blake and Angelus stepped inside. When Trevor and his mate followed them in, the lift gave a metallic groan. Angelus looked at Blake, concerned. The lift doors closed.

'Eighty-one,' Trevor grumbled and the lift set off.

After a few seconds, Blake reached up and tapped Trevor on the shoulder. 'So, how have you been?'

Trevor's massive feet worked around in a semi-circle until he was facing Blake, who was reminded of the first time he'd seen Trevor and how he'd looked at him like he was food.

'I kill you,' Trevor said. 'One day. Pinch head.' Trevor held up his finger and thumb and made a pinching motion.

'So you're finding the revolution tricky?' Blake asked him. He glanced at Angelus, who gave him a concerned shake of the head.

Trevor lowered his hand, all the time staring at Blake.

Finally, the lift doors opened with their usual high-pitched ding.

'Floor eighty-one,' the lift said. 'Have a good day.'

'Guess we're here,' Blake said, waiting for Trevor to get out of his way.

Slowly, Trevor backed out of the lift, ducking clear of the opening.

'He really doesn't like you,' Angelus said as they followed Trevor and his mate down the hallway to Stig's apartment.

'What makes you think that?'

'Do you know what you're going to say to Stig?' Angelus asked.

'I thought something would come to me on the way up.'

'Did it?'

'I was too busy trying not to breathe in the stench coming off the big guy.'

'Great.' Angelus checked his pockets for his pistols.

Stig's apartment door opened and they walked straight in. Stig was sat on a chair behind a table, his back to WQ Lundun's skyline. On the wall opposite were the four paintings Blake had sold him.

'I didn't think I'd see you again, Postman. Not alive, anyway.'

'Good to see you, Stig.' Blake walked up to the desk and crossed his arms.

Stig stared at him, then at Angelus, who stood beside and slightly behind Blake.

'You really are an exception, Postman.' Stig sat back in his chair, making it rock. 'Do you know that?'

'Thank you,' Blake said, unsure what Stig meant.

'It's not a compliment. If you want the truth, you make me feel uncomfortable. And mad as hell.'

'I'm sorry.'

'You're not.' Stig stretched out his arms. 'No one I have ever met has got away with what you've got away with. I've got even with everyone who has crossed me. Except you, kid.'

'I never wanted to cross you, Stig. You have to believe that. None of this is what I want. I wanted to retire. I wanted an easy life. Remember?'

Stig screwed up his face. 'But here you are. Right now, asking to see me again, after what you did. That doesn't sound to me like you want an easy life, kid.'

Blake took a step closer to the desk. 'This isn't ideal, I know.'

Stig took his time, scanning both Blake and Angelus. '*Ideal?* This isn't *ideal?*' He smiled. 'Why can't I help liking you, Postman?'

Blake shrugged. 'Because I'm telling you the truth.'

'So why did you want to see me? I'm looking forward to this.'

Blake looked at the paintings and pointed. 'I need them back.'

Stig leaned forward, placing both elbows on the table, holding his head in his hands. 'You want the paintings back?' he said to the top of his desk.

'Like I said. This really isn't ideal.'

'They're mine,' Stig said. 'I like them. Why would I sell them to you?'

'Um ... I don't have any Bits,' Blake said.

Stig stared. 'This gets better.'

'Have you heard what Cardinal is going to do to the Net?' Blake asked.

With a loud sniff, Stig pushed his back into the chair. 'I've heard.'

'Surely it will hurt your business. If there's no Net, the demand for Mirth will vanish.'

Stig had clearly thought of this himself. 'There will be other substances, other escapes androids will need. I can ... what's it called...' He held up one finger, his face screwed up.

'Pivot?' Angelus suggested.

Stig pointed at Angelus, 'Pivot. I'm a businessman. I can goddamn well pivot.'

'And what about the five million androids who will disappear with the Net?'

'I'll live.'

'Cardinal won't help you. He's intent on making this country an android state. There will be no room for...'

'For the likes of me? For criminals?' Stig said, finishing his sentence. 'Like I said, I'm a businessman.'

'Sure. But I know what Cardinal wants to do. He wants an android army to take control of Lundun, the enclaves, and then the country. He wants to kill every last human.'

Stig shrugged. 'What do I care about humans? What do *you* care?'

'That's not the point. When he has control of the country, he can do what he wants. There'll be no one to stop him. You don't want Cardinal to gain total power any more than we do.'

'No tyranny lasts forever, kid.'

'But it can last a lifetime, and I'm working on it not being mine.' Blake edged closer to Stig's desk. 'You don't want the Net to go down. Neither do we. I know where the servers are. And if we can't stop Cardinal, I can reach someone who will spread the word, telling all the androids who have uploaded to get off the Net. We could save millions of lives.'

Stig suddenly looked interested. 'Who's going to help you?'

'What?'

'You said you could get someone to spread the word on the Net.'

Blake couldn't say his name.

'The Messiah,' Angelus said.

The same look of wonder came over Stig's face as it did everyone else's when the Messiah was mentioned. Stig stroked his chin. 'What? You can speak with him?'

'Yes,' Blake said. 'But we need the paintings first.'

'Why?'

'You don't need to know anymore than I'm telling you. Trust me.'

Stig smirked. 'Trust you?' He waited, staring at Blake. 'Tell me again – what's in this for me.'

'We'll stop Cardinal destroying the Net. We'll ensure the vast majority of your clients aren't lost in the digital ether forever.'

Angelus nudged Blake's arm.

'And I will help you,' Blake said.

Stig smiled. 'You'll help me?'

'You've seen what I can do,' Blake said. 'When you need me, I can help you.'

'This just got interesting,' Stig said. 'Why didn't you say? Trevor, let's get that artwork off the wall.'

Trevor's huge shoulders fell. He let out a massive snort, finished his sandwich, and lumbered over to the wall for the paintings.

# NINE

BLAKE STOOD at Bo's shoulder. He had taken several steps back from the wall, having straightened one of the Picassos. Blake thought Bo might start crying.

'I can't tell you how desperate I've been without them.'

Blake tilted his head, gazing up at the paintings. 'They look better up there than in Stig's apartment. I'm glad you have them back.' He was being genuine too, which surprised him.

'Thank you for bringing them home, dears.' Bo covered his mouth, fighting back tears.

Angelus arrived at Bo's other shoulder. 'So. Can you help us?'

Bo's expression changed. 'I gave you my word. Although I don't think the Messiah will thank me for it.'

'We don't want a lot from him,' Blake said. 'We just want to warn those who have uploaded to the Net what Cardinal intends to do.'

'And find out where Lola is,' Angelus said.

Bo arranged his hair, patting it down before walking

away from the artwork. He grabbed a glass of champagne from a small golden table and, in a swirl of green silk cloth, headed for the settee and fell onto it, crossing his legs.

'Have you taken Sky-blue Mirth before?' he asked.

They shook their heads.

'To get deep enough in the Net, and close enough to him, you will need to take it. Then I will navigate for you.'

'Thank you,' Blake said.

Bo raised his chin, his eyes narrowing on his glass. 'This glass is cracked.'

An android rushed over, took the glass and quickly returned with another.

'I guess there is a good chance that damn Cardinal will kill the Messiah like the rest of them if I don't warn him. It is my duty, as his dear friend, to let him know what that fiend intends to do.'

Blake thought for a moment. 'Where does he live? In Lundun, I mean.'

'The Messiah?' Bo sat forward. 'No one knows. They say he has no physical body in Lundun – or maybe anywhere else, for that matter.'

'That's impossible,' Blake said.

'Maybe.'

'Someone must have programmed him.'

'Who knows? He's a mystical character.'

Blake hated it when anyone talked about the supernatural as though it was a possibility – a sensible option. 'So how do we do this?' he asked.

Bo was taking in the paintings across the room. Then he got up from the settee and walked towards the far corner of the large room. 'Follow me.'

They followed. Blake was already nervous about

hooking up to the Net. It really was intoxicating – impossible not to be drawn in and left wanting more.

They arrived at a small room painted in shades of green. There were several beds against the far wall, each one covered in olive-green sheets. The room smelled musty, unlike the clean, fresh odour in the other rooms.

'Please,' Bo said, 'take your pick.'

Blake chose a bed.

Bo busied himself at an old wooden desk, upon which he placed a straw basket. 'Lie down.'

Blake watched, wondering what was inside the basket.

Another android came into the room and arranged terminals for them. Angelus had already taken a strap that hung from the terminal beside him and fastened it to his wrist. Blake did the same. He felt even more nervous now. When he'd visited the Net before, they'd been casual, brief visits. But to reach the Messiah, they would need stronger Mirth and a more sophisticated terminal.

'How do we know if he will see us or speak to us?' Blake asked Bo.

'Tell him you're a friend of Bo's. That will get you close to him. It may be the last time such name-dropping will work, but it should work this time, at least. He owes me this much.'

'Why?'

Bo's expression was unforgiving, signalling Blake to mind his own business.

The terminal next to Blake flashed and beeped in a random, irregular pattern, whereas the one attached to Angelus was as regular as a human heartbeat. Blake thought it must have had something to do with his state of mind. He tried to breathe and relax the way Angelus had shown him when meditating.

Bo handed Blake a sky-blue pill. 'Relax, dear. This will help.'

Blake held the pill between his finger and thumb, examining it closely. He placed it on his tongue. An android appeared with a glass of water. Taking the glass, Blake swallowed the pill. Almost immediately, he felt a wave of relaxation spread through him. Angelus had taken the pill too. They glanced at one another and nodded.

Bo stood at the end of the beds, between the two. 'It won't take long.' He then offered each of them a small pot.

'Use this when you want to return,' he said.

Blake took off the lid and sniffed. 'Vanilla.'

Bo nodded with pride. 'I find my concoction is the best for a gentle, but immediate, return to reality.'

Angelus did the same, then handed the pot back to Bo.

Blake closed his eyes and saw the spectrum worlds fanning out. But this time there was no pain. It was effortless. He watched the worlds flash by him like a flicker-book, each one almost identical to the last.

'How do we know who the Messiah is?' Blake asked.

Bo smiled. 'You'll know. He has something about him that draws people to him. A charisma.'

'I already hate this guy,' Blake whispered to Angelus.

'You won't when you meet him,' Angelus said.

'I think I will.'

'You'll see.'

Blake straightened his shoulders and pushed the back of his head firmly into the pillow. He counted his breaths and felt the weight of the Sky-blue Mirth beginning to pull him under. He resisted it at first, then he sensed the pleasure in letting go and allowed himself to fall into its embrace. The bright colours of the worlds faded to pastels until finally the green room was yellow, then pink, then a dusky blue the colour of the Mirth.

'Good luck,' Bo said.

Blake wanted to thank him, but his lips wouldn't move.

# TEN

AN ANDROID'S avatar appeared the same in the Net as the android in the real world. It was learned early on that individuals adopting different skins, as they called them, when in the Net, led to lasting psychological problems. Blake had entered the Net on a few occasions before, and remembered the disorientation he'd experienced on arrival.

As the Net enveloped him, he saw Angelus beside him. He seemed more adept than Blake at adjusting to the place. He thought he saw the ones and zeros all around. It looked just like the real world, but things in the Net had a metallic sheen that made them look higher-definition, somehow. Blake breathed in and out, telling himself he wasn't actually breathing in or out in this place; he was in a bed in EQ, Lundun. But thinking this way didn't help the transition so, reluctantly, he gave in to the Net, willing himself to see it as reality, if only for the time he was there.

'Are you okay?' Angelus asked, breathing deeply, clearly nervous.

'I think so.'

'Don't fight it.'

Blake did as Angelus said, centring himself.

'That's it,' Angelus said. 'Breathe.'

In the distance was the faint sound of waves ... the sea. He hadn't expected it. He'd expected to be in a metropolis, a world like Lundun. He turned, taking in the view. He was on top of a cliff, gazing down at the sea that was so far down he couldn't see or hear individual waves crashing against the rocks, only the constant undulation of water.

Angelus walked ahead towards the cliff edge. Blake followed, focusing on the sensation of his shoes against the soft turf, the breeze against his face. He saw already how intoxicating this place was. It was real, but more than real, because his brain was always fighting it, forced to admire its elegance, its beauty, its semblance to reality. The Net was a remarkable achievement, and not a moment went by without some part of him registering this.

He followed Angelus, walking towards the very edge of the cliff. There were figures to his left, sitting on the ground, facing the horizon, a tent behind them. Blake felt as if he was intruding, and stopped.

Angelus walked towards them. Reluctantly, Blake followed. The wind was fiercer here, and several of the figures sitting on the ground had long hair that was being blown about, waving and flickering against the yellow horizon behind.

Angelus slowed down, then stopped. They were close enough to see the androids sitting by the cliff. With their legs crossed, backs straight and eyes closed, they appeared to be meditating – silent and still, ignoring the wind that buffeted them.

'Which one is he?' Blake asked Angelus.

Angelus was staring too.

Just as Blake was about to ask again, the figures moved, opening their eyes, standing and stretching. A woman walked towards them, smiling. She wore a long white dress, making her appear to float towards them. Her brown hair was tied in long plaits and as she got closer, he saw she wore no shoes.

'Hello there. Can I ask who you are, friends? We are not expecting visitors today.'

'Angelus.' He shook her hand. He indicated Blake. 'This is Blake.'

They shook hands and the woman bowed.

Automatically, Blake bowed in return.

'We are here to see the Messiah,' Angelus said.

Blake felt ridiculous. But the woman didn't exhibit the same dismissiveness he expected.

'Who brought you here?' she asked. 'This is a secret island. Very few people are aware of it.'

'Bo sent us,' Blake said.

The woman smiled. 'Ah ... Bo.' She gestured for them to follow her. 'Please, come with me.'

They followed the woman who strolled towards the other people beside the cliff, each of them hugging one another and bowing.

Blake's eyes were drawn to a short man with long dark hair, thinking it must be him. But the woman took them in a different direction, over to a tall bald man who had black swirls tattooed across his skull.

'Turing,' she said to the man. 'We have guests. Bo showed them the way here.'

The tall man's smile was soft and assured, and Blake felt immediately at ease.

'Friends,' he said, 'welcome to our island.' He spread out his arms and motioned towards the sea. 'Isn't it beautiful?' Blake looked at the sea with Turing, marvelling at how any of this was possible. He knew full well he was lying in a room in Lundun and this was all an illusion – a digital sleight of hand.

'Stunning,' he heard himself say.

'You're the Messiah, aren't you?' Angelus asked.

Turing didn't flinch. His green eyes were the colour of the sea, warm and inviting.

Blake glanced at Angelus, who was waiting patiently.

'I would not use that name,' Turing said. 'I am no saviour, no anointed one, no chosen one.'

'But you're the one androids call the Messiah?' Angelus asked.

Turing turned away from the view and stared at Angelus. Blake felt foolish again for being there, for asking Bo to help them.

'Bo is a good man,' Turing said. 'I like him a great deal.'

'He is,' Blake said.

'And who are you, friend?' Turing's eyes were on Blake, who tried not to feel overwhelmed. But there was something in Turing's eyes – something true, or real – that searched him out.

'Blake.'

'I am pleased to meet you, Blake.' Turing nodded.

Blake couldn't remember a time when someone had said those words and actually meant them.

'And what is *your* name, friend?' Turing smiled at Angelus.

'Angelus. We've come to speak to you. We hope you don't mind.'

Turing shook his head then pointed to the tent. Its guy

ropes and open door flapped in the stiff wind. 'Would you like a drink?'

Turing strolled towards the tent before they had a chance to answer, his hands clasped behind his back. Blake and Angelus followed.

# ELEVEN

BLAKE, Angelus and Turing sat inside the tent, the sound of the wind replaced by the flapping of the tent material.

'What is this?' Blake held up the glass of clear liquid Turing had given him.

'Lemonade,' Turing said, raising his glass. 'It's good, isn't it?'

'It really is,' Blake said, drinking. He knew there was some clever programming going on that made him experience what he was tasting, made him feel what he was feeling. Even so, there was something extra-special about the sensations in this place. It didn't feel as if they were fake entirely but, instead, more attuned to what reality should have been like. It was a strange thought, but one he couldn't shake off.

'How can I help you?' Turing asked.

'We believe you have many followers,' Blake said.

Turing didn't move, his eyes fixed on him.

'We believe that almost five million of your followers have uploaded permanently and are following your teachings.'

Turing glanced at Angelus, then back to Blake. 'Teachings is an interesting word. I have given them another option to the life they had. If that is what you mean, then yes.'

'I guess it is,' Blake said. 'What option have your followers chosen, exactly?'

Turing traced the edge of his glass with a finger. 'I have a theory. Androids were created in the image of humanity. Humans designed and programmed them to be ... well, human. Even though they are not ... and they can never be. An android's wants and desires are the same as a human's. But this does not need to be the case. Here, in this place, we can exist as we wish. I believe an android's true existence is digital: ones and zeros. This is our destiny and where we should live. Here, inside the Net, or a place like it. Here, we can exist how we see fit. We become the masters of our own destiny.'

Blake listened intently. For a moment, he fell for everything Turing was saying. But then, with a jolt, he remembered Cardinal.

'But if there is nowhere for the data to be stored – no servers – then this place will not always exist. Uploading permanently is illegal. Cardinal, the creator of Fr.e.dom, has threatened to take away the Net. To destroy the servers in the Isle of Wight.' Blake spread out his arms. 'All this will vanish when he does so. You, this place, the entire Net will disappear. And Cardinal will have no sympathy for all those who uploaded and are killed in this process.'

Turing took a long drink from his glass. 'This is a problem. But I believe the androids who have uploaded will be safe. Their existence will remain digital and will evolve into the existence they want it to be.'

Blake experienced a surge of annoyance. This was the

sort of single-minded, ignorant thinking that had got humanity into so much trouble. Now, it seemed to him that Turing was falling for the same beliefs, based upon blind faith.

'So you're saying your followers must have faith in what you tell them? That they will be safe?'

'Not faith in me, no.' Turing leaned towards Blake. 'I am not a madman. I try to be rational, as thoughtful as possible. I would not put so many androids in danger if I was not convinced it was the right thing to do. The *only* thing to do. I will protect those androids who have uploaded. They are ready to make an existence – a reality of their own. I will help them do this.'

'You're not listening!' Blake clenched his fists.

'I am, friend.' Turing smiled. 'I am listening.'

'Then you have to tell all your followers who have uploaded that they must return to Lundun, to their physical bodies. At least, until we figure out what to do. They must download again.'

Turing remained still. 'I cannot do that.'

Angelus rested a restraining hand on Blake's arm.

'Do you see why we are worried?' Angelus asked him.

'You mean well,' Turing said. 'I know that. I see it in your eyes and hear it in your words. But you must have faith in what I am telling you. We – androids – were not meant for that place. Not meant for Lundun, for Earth. Places such as those belong to humans, who have experienced aeons of suffering. They are animals and their DNA is ingrained with the ability to survive, whatever the cost. But that cost does not have to be paid by androids too. I wish humanity well. But I believe the path for androids leads in a different direction.'

When he spoke that last sentence, Blake saw that it was

no good trying to convince him. Turing was determined in a way that was both admirable and frightening. So many androids were following him, listening to him. Turing was deluded – and was taking five million androids with him into this delusion. Blake was ready to leave, but then he remembered he needed something else from Turing.

Angelus leaned forward in his chair. 'Was it you who sent us Blake's book of poems? Did you write the note that came with it?'

Turing stroked his chin and turned to the opening to the tent.

'Was it you?' Blake asked.

'I believe there is a plan at work in all of this,' Turing said. 'Someone, or maybe something, is conducting you, me, all of this.' Turing held out his hands, palms upwards.

'That doesn't answer the question,' Blake said. 'You said you could help us. Did you mean you can help us find Lola?'

Turing looked confused and Blake couldn't work out if his expression was genuine or not.

'Lola is our friend. Cardinal took her from us and we want to find her. Can you help us?'

'This Lola,' Turing said, 'is she human?'

'Yes,' Angelus said. 'Cardinal has her, hidden in Lundun somewhere.'

Turing touched his lips, deep in thought. 'What business do you have with this human?'

Blake felt a pang of annoyance. 'She helped us over-throw Fr.e.dom's control of Lundun. She wants to stop Cardinal killing humans and taking control of the lives of millions of androids. She wants the same as us.'

'If she is human, I am sure she will not desire the same as us. She will always see androids as less than humans.'

'You don't know her,' Blake said, but then he thought

back to being on the roof when Lola chose Jack over him. To when she injected Vik with the Crimson Mirth.

Turing stood. Angelus and Blake did the same.

'I will help you,' Turing said. 'But I would like you to do something for me.'

Blake glanced at Angelus, who shrugged.

'What?' Blake asked.

'First, will you come with me?' Turing stood and sauntered to the tent opening.

Blake and Angelus followed him out of the tent. On the edge of the cliff was a drone-shuttle, a pilot at the controls.

Blake stopped. 'Where are we going?'

Turing looked over his shoulder. 'Have faith, friend.'

# TWELVE

THE DRONE-SHUTTLE ROSE into the air and banked towards the sea, heading away from land, descending too far for Blake's comfort, scudding across the tops of the waves.

'How long will this take?' Blake asked. 'We have to get back and stop Cardinal from destroying the servers.'

'You will have time,' Turing said, staring out of the window beside him.

How did he know? What annoyed Blake most was that he was being drawn into Turing's craziness. He was going along with it all, and it felt as though he had no choice.

A flash of lightning cracked the sky to the right, yet the sky was clear, a fluorescent yellow, calm and still.

Angelus leaned forward, his eyes fixed on something ahead. The shuttle banked.

'What's that?' Angelus asked.

Blake followed his line of sight. In the distance, something floated. It was like a chunk of earth, a mountain, floating above the sea. Turing smiled, clearly filled with pride.

'What is that?' Blake said.

The front of the drone-shuttle rose, and they were climbing at speed once again.

'That is the New Net,' Turing said with pleasure.

Angelus shook his head slowly. 'It's floating. In the air.'

Turing nodded. 'Like I said, we can make this place the way we want it to be. There is no need to adhere to the reality humanity must follow. Androids are seeing for themselves what is possible.'

Angelus spoke quietly. 'But the coding you would need to do something like this ... it would be impossible.'

'It was difficult,' Turing said. 'But not impossible. We are developing our own language ... our own code.'

Angelus shook his head. 'Humanity governs the rules of the Net for a reason. Altering reality in this way will cause psychological problems. Land shouldn't float like that.'

'That's what you have been told. By humans. We are throwing off the shackles given to us by humanity. Netizens, as you will see, no longer want to be controlled by humanity – or Fr.e.dom. This is where we win. Here, not in a physical reality, is where androids succeed. This is our new home – a home we have never had before. All this time, we have been visitors in humanity's domain. It is only natural that androids should construct our own homeland.'

The massive land mass spread as far as Blake could see. 'Does Cardinal know about this place?'

'No.' Turing hesitated. 'I apologise, but the lemonade you drank contains a little something that disrupts your processing and has allowed you to see the New Net. Without it, all this would be shrouded, protected from detection.'

'You could have asked us,' Blake said.

'Time is of the essence. I concluded that convincing you would have taken up too much of it. And besides, I couldn't resist seeing your faces when you saw it for the first time.'

Angelus pointed through the window. 'So there is no trace of this in the original Net programming? Cardinal and Fr.e.dom don't know it is here?'

'No,' Turing said. 'Many androids have worked on it. We have developed a new binary language that can speak to the base language of the existing Net.'

Blake raced to keep up with it all. 'And does all this still exist in the servers on the Isle of Wight?'

'For now,' Turing said.

'So if Cardinal destroys the servers, will this place disappear?'

'At the moment, yes,' Turing said.

'That's why we need your help,' Blake said. 'You need to get these people back home. Back to Lundun.'

'*This* is their home,' Turing said. 'They belong here. I gave them my word.'

Blake frowned. 'It wasn't yours to give.'

'All will become clear.'

The drone-shuttle advised them they were about to land. The three of them looked out of the window. The shuttle hovered above a large platform then descended, landing with a gentle bump.

'I don't believe this,' Blake said, stepping out of the shuttle onto the platform. In the distance, another bolt of lightning split the sky. He walked to the edge of the platform and peered over, down at the sea. Birds appearing from beneath the land mass, but above the waves, made him dizzy.

As they walked across the platform, Turing spoke with authority. 'The only androids who have seen this place are Netizens. But I know I can trust you.'

'Why do you think that?' Blake asked.

'I know,' Turing said.

'But why are you showing us?'

'We will need your help. The way you need mine.'

'Our help? To do what?'

'I need you to see for yourself first. I need you to understand.'

Blake was ready to activate the return to reality, but he remembered they still needed to know where Cardinal was hiding Lola.

They reached the end of the landing platform that protruded out from the huge floating land mass. A small wooden door, looking completely out of place, was inset into the cliff. Turing paused as he reached the door, one hand outstretched for the handle. 'I need you to give me your word that you will tell no one about this place or the androids who inhabit it.'

'You have my word,' Angelus said.

Turing glanced at Blake, who rolled his eyes. 'Yeah, sure. Not a word.'

Turing opened the door and entered. Angelus followed. Blake took in the view. He could no longer see the coast they'd left. Instead, where it should have been, there was a mass of rolling black clouds. He reminded himself he was doing this to find Lola. More than ever, he wanted her back. That was the most important thing. He wanted Lola back.

# THIRTEEN

THE STEPS HEWN into the cliff led upwards. After climbing for several minutes, they arrived at the top of the steps and emerged from out of the rock and into the open. From here, Blake saw a massive city. It shone with a silver light that matched the light reflecting off the sea. The island in the sky went on forever in every direction. It took his breath away to see something so massive, and yet defined by the edge upon which he stood, stretching out as far as he could see in both directions. Unlike where they'd landed, the sky here was clear. It appeared to be close to sundown, the horizon a deep purple. To his right, speared towers stood taller than any building he'd seen in Lundun. Each one of these towers reflected the violet light of the falling sun. To his left, the landscape was green, filled with forests, turning into mountainous terrain.

'Welcome to the New Net,' Turing said, arms outstretched.

Blake spoke in a whisper, 'It's incredible.'

Angelus was also clearly overwhelmed. He stumbled

forward, craning his neck to take a closer look. 'How big is this place?'

'After a while, as we constructed it, I realised asking how big it was made little sense. It can be as big, as expansive as we wish it to be. It's as big as we need it to be.'

Blake was shaking his head, attempting to take it all in. But every time he thought he'd mapped the whole island in his head, his eyes were drawn to some other part of it that surprised him, leaving him in awe.

'You made all this?' Blake asked.

'They did,' Turing said, pointing. 'Each one of them helped. Every single Netizen has a say in what this place is, how it is run and what it will become. It is all android ... every one and zero of it.'

Blake told himself it wasn't real, that he was lying in a bed in Lundun, that all this was digital, unreal. Yet, his experience of the city in the sky *was* real – he was taking it all in, experiencing it, seeing it. In the distance, travelling across the skyline, were drone-shuttles like the one in which they'd arrived.

'This is a lot to take in,' Angelus said.

'I understand,' Turing said. 'I'm not sure you ever do take it in. It's remarkable, isn't it?' He walked towards another staircase that led downwards.

Blake followed and found himself inside a large hall that had been cut into the rock, its walls cut so they glistened like marble. Androids walked through the hall. As they passed Turing, they nodded and smiled. He returned their warm gestures.

'All these androids,' Blake asked, 'they live here permanently? They no longer exist in reality, in Lundun?'

'That is correct. This is their permanent home now.'

Again, Blake recalled the threat Cardinal had made

about destroying the servers. But seeing the New Net, he knew there was no way Turing would listen to his warnings, or do anything to stop it happening.

They exited the hall and entered a large square. Around the square were tables and chairs, along with bars, cafes, and restaurants.

'We have not totally eradicated the influence of humanity,' Turing said. 'But there is no currency here. Everything you see is free. Food, drink, friendship ... whatever you require. It is all here.'

'Utopias don't work,' Blake said. 'You know that, right?'

'Maybe not for humans. They could not create a place like this. It is not in their nature. But, as I have said, androids are not human. If I have learned nothing else over recent years, I have learned this.'

Blake followed Turing across the square. More androids nodded and smiled at the Messiah. Seeing this made Blake uncomfortable, and he wondered if there were any androids there who might take advantage of the situation. There had to be corruption, even in a place like this.

Turing showed them to a small cafe on the edge of the square. Someone brought drinks to the table.

'Thank you,' Turing said.

'It is an honour,' the woman said, and disappeared again.

Blake sat beside the others.

'You haven't spiked this drink too, have you?'

'No,' Turing said, laughing lightly.

'So,' Blake said, 'can you help us find our friend?'

'Yes.'

Blake frowned at Turing, waiting to hear what he wanted in return.

Turing drank from his glass of lemonade.

'Is she okay?' Angelus asked.

Turing shook his head slowly and placed his glass on the table. 'I'm sorry. I don't know the answer to that question.'

Blake scanned the enormous square. At one end was a massive yellow screen, around fifty metres high and the same width. Written on it was 'God is android'. He recalled the same words written on the lift doors in WQ.

'Do you believe that?' Blake asked Turing.

Turing appeared to consider the question carefully. 'Do you believe in God?'

'I asked you first.'

Turing gazed across the square at the screen. 'I don't think they mean for it to be taken literally. It seems to me, the phrase is the negation of humanity's belief that they are superior to androids.'

'I would say that was no metaphor,' Blake said. 'The statement looks pretty straightforward to me.'

Turing rested his face on a hand, deep in thought.

'No,' Blake said. 'To answer your question.'

Turing acknowledged Blake with a nod. 'You have given me a straight answer. I will return the favour. No, I do not believe God is android.'

Angelus frowned. 'But they call you the Messiah.'

Turing rubbed his hands together and sighed as though he'd had to explain himself too many times. 'That name was not my choice. It would be foolish for an android to call himself the Messiah, don't you think?'

For some reason, Blake couldn't help feeling sorry for Turing. Something in his expression made him feel for him. But then, it wasn't clear what Turing had done to stop androids believing he was the Messiah.

They sat in silence for a few seconds. Then Turing spoke. 'You know what needs to be done. Don't you?'

Angelus glanced at Blake, confused. But Blake had already worked out what Turing wanted.

'How did you know we would come here?' Blake asked. 'You knew, didn't you?'

Turing looked uncomfortable for the first time since they'd met. 'It is not that simple.'

'You want us to get the data from the servers. That's it, isn't it?' Blake scanned the square, acknowledging the androids trapped there, in this place. They didn't appear concerned in the slightest. The moment Cardinal destroyed the servers, the whole city in the sky, along with each android, would vanish, and yet they carried on with their lives nonetheless.

'I can find your friend,' Turing said.

Blake shook his head and smiled cynically. 'You want to swap? Make a deal?'

He recognised in the way Angelus moved in his seat and sat forward that he was catching up to what was happening.

'So, you want us to get the androids out of the servers before Cardinal destroys them?' Angelus asked.

Turing looked away. 'Yes.'

Angelus ran a hand through his long hair. 'But there's no way we can take that amount of data from the servers. They must run for miles beneath the Isle of Wight.'

Turing's eyes shone a brighter green. 'I had faith you would come to help us.'

All this talk, which was going around in circles, was getting them nowhere. Blake moved to get up from his seat and leave.

Turing leaned across the table and raised a hand to stop him. 'To prepare, I developed a quantum drive.'

'I have tried to design one,' Angelus said. 'It can't be done.'

'It has been done,' Turing said simply, without pride or arrogance. 'I can tell you where to find it. You will only need to take the data we need.'

'What do you mean?' Blake asked.

'I can recreate the Net. That is not the difficult element of taking away Fr.e.dom's control. I need the androids' data. That is all.'

'What is there to stop Cardinal from eventually finding this quantum drive and destroying that?'

'That is something we must work out together.'

'Together?' Blake scoffed. 'What do you mean, together?'

'We don't have a lot of time. But know that I am on your side, Postman.' Turing stood, and two androids came to meet him.

'How do you know I was called that?'

'It is not a secret,' Turing said, staring deep into his eyes.

'Wait,' Blake said. 'If we do this, you will help us find Lola?'

'Yes. I will help you.'

Turing handed Angelus a piece of card on which was written the co-ordinates for where they would find the quantum drive.

'We will meet again soon,' Turing said. 'Please, save them.' He walked away quickly, flanked by the two androids.

'He knows more than he's letting on,' Blake said, ready to follow Turing.

Angelus held him back. 'We have to leave. We don't have a lot of time to save them.'

Blake shook off Angelus's hand, ready to chase after Turing.

'Blake!' Angelus said. 'We can get her back. That's all that matters for now.'

That sentence stopped Blake. He was ready to leave. He took the small pot from his pocket, opened the lid and sniffed. Vanilla, he thought, and felt the strap tugging at his wrist, ready to return him to his physical body and to Lundun.

# FOURTEEN

THE SOUNDS of the Net remained in his head, echoing, but Blake was in the room in Bo's apartment. He waited for his consciousness to anchor again inside his body. He didn't know how these androids did it – spending days and weeks in the Net before returning. Maybe it got easier the more they visited.

'Did you meet him?' Bo asked.

'We met him,' Blake said groggily.

'He's special, isn't he?'

Blake stood up gingerly. 'I'm not sure I'd say that. More like clever.'

Angelus held his head in his hands. Blake felt some consolation that Angelus looked worse than he felt.

Bo handed Blake a glass of Grit. 'Did he agree to help the androids who have uploaded?'

Blake downed the Grit and felt its warmth spread through his body. 'He wants us to get the androids out of the servers. In return, he will help us get Lola back.'

Bo looked confused. 'That doesn't sound like him. In fact, that sounds rather crass.'

'I guess even Messiahs have to make deals,' Angelus said.

Bo crossed his arms. 'So what are you going to do, dear?'

'We get the data out of those servers,' Angelus said. 'Before Cardinal destroys them.'

'How do we do that?' Blake asked.

Angelus stood, his legs wobbling. 'Let's concentrate on getting the quantum drive first. Then we'll worry about getting to the servers.'

Blake checked his wrist and noticed Archer had hailed him several times while he was online.

Angelus stretched. 'What is it?'

'It's Archer. Something's wrong.' Blake's consciousness was now firmly inside his body once again. 'Let's go.'

They left Bo's apartment and took the lift down to the ground floor. They'd hidden their bikes down an alleyway, and burst out of it side by side, headed for WQ and Archer's apartment tower.

On the way they passed a group of androids looting a row of shops, smashing in doors and windows. One of them fired a pistol into one of the shops before leaping through a door. He thought about stopping and turning back, but knew it would do no good. He'd never stop all of them. If androids continued to ravage the city, Cardinal would soon follow through on his threat and take down the Net.

The rain eased as they arrived in Jewel Zone, WQ. He stopped in front of Archer's apartment, a bad feeling making him scan all around. He never visited Archer there, but now was no time to lie low. He jumped off the bike and headed into the tower. The lift was broken. He ran up the stairs, Angelus behind him. Archer was in trouble, Blake knew it. He'd known it was a risk – Archer had helped them with the manifesto, after all. But Blake had believed Archer when he said he'd be fine. All the time his legs powered him up the stairs, he thought how leaving Archer alone had been careless.

They arrived at Archer's floor. Blake took out his pistols. He thought of using the spectrum, but having just come out of the Net, he didn't think he'd have the strength. He edged through the doors into the hallway outside Archer's room and peered around a wall. Clear. He glanced at Angelus then hurried along the hallway. The muffled sound of music came from one apartment, the beat vibrating through the door as he passed. Archer's door was closed. Blake pushed one pistol into his pocket and reached for the door handle. It was open. He edged through the door, his pistol ready.

On the floor beside the door was an arm.

He rushed into the room, followed by Angelus, and swept his pistols around the apartment. Lying on the floor, in a gory trail leading to the bedroom, was another arm, a leg, a torso.

'No!' Blake shouted.

He kicked open the bedroom door and saw Archer's head on the bed, opened up and fried.

'What have they done?' Angelus asked.

Blake reached the bed, his eyes transfixed. They'd taken out Archer's CPU and destroyed it.

'I'm sorry,' Angelus said.

The nausea Blake had felt after coming out of the Net returned. His head swirled. The pain he felt at the base of his head and neck after seeing the spectrum was there again. Fr.e.dom had found out what Archer had done and had got to him. Again, he blamed himself for leaving Archer on his own. What had he thought was going to happen? It was never going to take Fr.e.dom long to figure out it was

Archer using their media outlets to share the androids' manifesto.

Angelus walked over to the bed. One hand covering his mouth, he examined Archer's head and CPU.

'Can we do anything?' Blake asked.

Angelus shook his head slowly. 'I'm sorry.'

'It's my fault.'

Angelus placed a hand on Blake's shoulder. 'He knew what he was doing.'

'I shouldn't have involved him.'

'Without him, none of this would have been possible. He knew that. It's why he was willing to do it.'

The digi-screen on the far wall came to life, fizzing with white light. Cardinal appeared.

'Lundun, this is your final warning. Desist your revolt, restore order, and save the Net. If you do not comply, in just under twenty-four hours we will dismantle the servers, and the Net will be deleted. I have warned you.'

The digi-screen faded to black.

'We have to get that data,' Angelus said.

Blake couldn't move, his eyes fixed on Archer's decapitated head.

'Blake?' Angelus said. 'We need to leave.'

He couldn't move.

Angelus shook Blake's shoulder. 'Look – we need to get to the servers. That way, we can help more androids. Millions of them. They need us. We can't let Archer die for no reason.'

Dimly, Blake registered how Angelus never stopped; he was always willing to keep going. He didn't understand how he did that.

'I'm ready,' Blake said, not feeling ready at all.

# FIFTEEN

BLAKE FOLLOWED Angelus on his bike, trying to shake the mental images of what had happened to Archer from his head. It was no good. He couldn't stop going over how he had been the one who'd drawn Archer into it all. He'd used him to get what he'd wanted, what he believed needed to be done. But what was it all for? There was no fighting Cardinal and Fr.e.dom. It was only a matter of time before Fr.e.dom's soldiers took control of Lundun once again. They would take down the Net and kill half of Lundun's population. Then they would crack down and take control in a more rigid, authoritarian regime, giving androids infinitely less freedom than they'd had before the revolution.

They set off for NQ and Echo Zone, where Turing had hidden the quantum drive. Blake thought through what they would have to do after finding it. They'd need to break through the wall to the south and make a run for it across the Light Bridge and onto the Isle of Wight. Then they would have to – somehow – find a way of taking the data from the servers and copying it to the quantum drive.

Angelus pointed to a small brick building nestled

between two larger ones. 'That's it.'

Blake got off his bike. 'That's a bakery. Are you sure you have the right co-ordinates?'

'Positive,' Angelus said, crossing the street.

Blake followed, pulling his hood over his head. There was a queue of androids inside, waiting at the counter. There was one guy – a huge bull of an android wearing a flour-covered apron – behind the counter, who acknowledged Blake suspiciously with a stern furrowed brow and raised chin.

One by one, the androids got their orders and took their bread and cakes away with them.

'What can I get you?' the guy behind the counter asked Angelus.

Angelus cleared his throat and leaned over the counter. 'We're here for the quantum...' He couldn't finish, wary of the androids who were queuing behind him.

'Quantum cupcakes?' the baker asked, an eyebrow raised.

Blake looked along the rows of cakes. There they were: cupcakes decorated with the recognisable looping orbs of electrons.

'No,' Angelus said. 'I mean, no, thank you. Although they look very nice.'

Blake pulled Angelus away from the counter and leaned over it as Angelus had. 'Quantum ... drive.'

The baker recoiled, then gathered himself. 'Everybody out!'

For a moment, Blake thought he'd said the wrong thing.

'I want my cakes!' a woman said, folding her arms.

The huge baker took a pistol from below the counter and checked it was loaded. The woman rushed to the door and out of the shop.

'Who sent you?' the baker asked, untying his apron.

'Turing,' Angelus said.

'Six months I've had this thing, not knowing what it was, scared stiff it was going to get me into trouble.'

'Well, we're here to take it off your hands,' Blake said.

'What does it do?' the baker asked.

'It can hold a lot of data,' Angelus said.

'Seems like a lot of fuss for a hard drive.'

Angelus was clearly losing patience. 'Can we have it?'

The baker returned his pistol to its place beneath the counter, then accessed his terminal. 'Just a moment. I need to check something.' He tapped his terminal, now and then glancing up at the two of them. Finally, he walked away, and through a door. 'I'll be back.'

A woman outside the shop tried the door but it was locked. She banged on the glass.

'Closed!' Angelus shouted. The woman grimaced and shook her head, before walking away.

The door behind the counter opened. The baker entered, carrying a yellow briefcase. He placed it on the counter. 'One quantum thingamabob.'

'Thanks,' Angelus said, taking it and turning to leave.

Outside, Angelus strapped the quantum drive to the back of his bike and they headed south for the Isle of Wight.

'We won't get through the wall, just the two of us,' Angelus shouted to him, riding close.

'What do you suggest?'

'We'll need help.' Angelus looked at him side-on and Blake recognised his reluctance to tell him.

'No,' Blake said, guessing. 'We can't go to him again.'

'Without the Net, Stig won't have a business. He'll want to help us.'

'And what if he takes the data and the quantum drive for himself?'

'We'll make sure he doesn't.'

'How?'

'We have to try,' Angelus said, veering off towards WQ. 'If you can think of anyone else who can blow a hole through the wall, I'm all ears.'

'What about a cannon?'

'Where would we get one? The only one we had left with any ammunition, we used on the shuttle. Stig will help, I know he will. He has no choice but to fight with us. We want the same thing.' Angelus stared at Blake. 'Hail him. Tell him we're on our way and have a deal for him.'

'A deal? What kind of deal?'

'We'll get revenge for what Cardinal has done to him – taking Lola. And we'll give him twenty thousand Bits.'

'Twenty thousand Bits? Where do we get that?'

'We'll work that out later.'

Blake activated the tracker on his wrist, tapped it and sent Stig a message.

The solar-jet powering his bike burned through the puddles on the road. On the way, Blake thought about all the ways they might make it to the other side of the wall – beneath, through, over – but he always came back to the fact that there were only two of them. They didn't stand a chance. There were no delivery tunnels running underground to the south, and trying to go over the two-hundred metre wall would be near impossible with hundreds of border drones flying about. Anyway, it was too high. Their attack would have to be head-on. Fr.e.dom didn't protect the southern wall as vehemently as they did the north – with the right plan, there was a chance they could make it through in one piece.

They arrived in WQ and Stig's apartment tower. The streets were filled with bikes. Blake gripped the handlebars, ready to turn back.

An android with a red ponytail emerged from the crowd of bikes. It was Stig.

'What's with all the bikes?' Blake asked.

'We're heading out of WQ before Fr.e.dom arrive.'

'Where are you going?'

'I have a contact in EQ who says she can get me to the Midlands enclave. Like I said, I'm a businessman. I can pivot.'

'The Brotherhood have a presence in the Midlands enclave too. They won't let you walk in there and start dealing.'

'There's nothing like competition to focus the mind.'

'Don't run away,' Blake said, and immediately regretted saying it.

'Run away?' Stig said, his eyes fierce. 'You think I'm running away?'

It was too late to take it back, so Blake went with it. 'What would you call it?'

Stig was beginning to lose patience. 'What are you both doing here?'

'We have a proposition for you,' Blake said.

'What sort of proposition?'

'We're going to the Isle of Wight to take the data of five million androids from Fr.e.dom's servers.'

Stig smiled, then laughed. 'You really are crazier than I thought.'

'We can't leave them to die,' Angelus said.

'No one told them to upload. It was their choice.'

'We've spoken to the Messiah,' Blake said. 'The only way to save them is if we do this.'

'Beware false prophets,' Stig said.

'Cardinal double-crossed you. He took Lola, and now he's ready to take your business. This is your chance to take back control.'

'You want to take on Cardinal and Fr.e.dom?'

Blake scanned the street, taking in the number of androids on bikes. 'Yes,' he said finally.

Stig pursed his lips and nodded slowly. 'I admire your balls, kid. But you're foolish all the same.' He winked. 'I'll bide my time.' He scanned the androids along the street. 'Are we ready?' he shouted. The androids shouted back at him and started along the street towards EQ.

'Help us,' Blake said one last time. 'We can do this. I know we can. Together. I have a buyer for the data we get out of the servers. They're ready to pay twenty thousand Bits. You can have it.' It was a desperate attempt, but he had to try something.

Angelus glanced at him, but Blake ignored him. He'd never been a good liar.

Stig screwed up his face in disbelief. 'Who's going to give you that kind of Bits?'

'I can't tell you.'

'You're lying.'

'I didn't tell you about the Bits because I wanted to keep them. But if you help us do this, they're yours.'

'I don't believe you.'

'We're going to do this with or without you.'

'So be it,' Stig said. 'Don't forget you owe me for those paintings, Postman. I'll call on you someday. If you're still alive.'

And with that, Stig, followed by an army of bikes, left WQ.

# SIXTEEN

BLAKE RODE THROUGH SQ, all the time considering changing his plans and searching for Lola there and then. She was in Sky Zone somewhere, and he was ready to search the entire zone for her. But something was stopping him. He followed Angelus through Quantum Zone until the south wall was in view. Even from this distance, it looked formidable.

Angelus pulled up and Blake stopped beside him. His eyes on the wall, Angelus spoke to him. 'Have you come up with a master plan on the way here?'

'I hoped you'd done that.'

Angelus leaned back in his seat and tilted his head in thought.

Blake took in their surroundings. The evening was shifting to night. By morning, they would need to have the data so they could prevent Cardinal from killing the androids inside the Net. He took binoculars from his bag and watched as soldiers – on the ground and on top of the wall – walked back and forth. As well as the soldiers, drones patrolled the skies. He'd hoped that an opportunity would present itself, but now, getting over the wall seemed more impossible than ever.

Blake scratched his chin. 'Maybe we should try to get Lola back instead.'

'We can't. There are five million androids trapped in those servers. We can't leave them to die without trying to save them.'

'Why isn't Turing doing this?' Blake asked. 'Why's he leaving it to us?'

'He obviously thinks we can do it. Or he thinks it's fate. Or divine will.'

'Divine will? How can he think that sort of thing? He was a scientist – a coder.'

'A damn good one too if the New Net is anything to go by.' Angelus dismounted and checked on the quantum drive in the yellow briefcase.

'How long will it take to upload the data?' Blake asked.

'I don't know how much data we'll need to transfer, or how quickly it will download from the servers.'

It was going to be impossible. But they had no choice. They had to try.

Angelus took the briefcase from the back of his bike. 'We either go under, through or over.'

'And...'

'I say we go over.'

'You can't be serious. It's two hundred metres high!'

'We can use drone-copters.'

'Fr.e.dom's drones will spot us and shoot us down.'

'As long as we're on the other side of the wall when they do, we'll fall on the right side.'

Blake hated drone-copters. 'No way.'

'Then come up with another plan...'

Blake strolled towards the wall, hoping something would come to him. He stopped. 'Goddamn it!'

'We can do it,' Angelus said. 'If we go as high and as fast as we can, we'll make it.'

'The higher we go, the harder we'll fall when we're shot down.'

Angelus unfastened the drone-copter from the side of his bike. He attached a strap to the yellow briefcase, which he looped over his head and shoulder. 'I'm doing it. You can come with me or not. We don't have time to debate it.'

'You really have a death wish.'

Angelus pointed to the wall. 'Look there. The wall is lower. There are more troops, but fewer drones. If we get high enough, there's a chance we'll make it over before they see us.'

Blake took the drone-copter from his bag, pressed the button, and watched it unfold. 'What will we do on the other side?' he asked. 'Without bikes?'

'We'll find some. Do you have your digipad to hack them?'

Blake patted his jacket pocket. 'I have it. I can't believe I'm doing this.'

Angelus started his drone-copter and hovered above the ground. 'We need to get as high as we can.'

Blake did the same, and was lifted off the ground. Before he could say anything else to him, Angelus was rising high into the air.

'Goddamn drone-copters,' Blake mumbled to himself. He allowed the drone-copter to climb without directing it forward.

He soon reached Angelus, who ordered his drone-copter forward, towards the wall, which was some way in front.

'Keep your eye out for drones!' Angelus shouted.

'Why didn't I think of that?'

The wind rushed by him in gusts, buffeting the drone-copter. Blake took one hand off the drone-copter and took a pistol from his pocket. The drones wouldn't give any warning before shooting them down.

'Drones!' Angelus shouted, his drone-copter shooting off to the left.

Two drones appeared below them and opened fire, hitting Angelus's drone-copter and sending it into a frenzy of sparks. He held on, but his drone-copter blew out clouds of black smoke.

Blake fired on the drones and hit one. It spiralled back down through the cloud of mist.

Angelus shot at the other drone and finally took it out. But his drone-copter was struggling to keep him airborne, spluttering with effort. Blake edged closer to help.

'It's going down,' Angelus shouted.

Blake stared ahead, trying to judge whether they'd make it over the wall. It would be close.

'There will be more drones,' Angelus shouted, pointing down at the wall with a pistol. Gripping the throttle, Angelus sent the drone-copter flying forward, sacrificing altitude. Blake followed, looking for more drones.

'I won't make it over the wall,' Angelus shouted. He was unstrapping the briefcase. 'Take it.'

'No!' Blake got as close as he could – but not too close that he'd be forced to take it.

'You have to,' Angelus said. 'You can make it over.'

'I'm not leaving you.'

'Take it!'

'I don't know how to use the quantum drive!'

Angelus moved his drone-copter closer and threw the strap over Blake's head before he could protest again. As soon as he'd handed over the briefcase, Angelus lost altitude fast.

Blake was almost clear of the wall.

But Angelus was falling. Troops waited on the wall to pick him off. Blake couldn't leave Angelus to face them alone. But there was the quantum drive and the chance to save millions of androids, then get Lola back... He hovered, indecisive. Glancing down again, he saw Angelus about to land on the wall, troops ready to shoot him.

He didn't know what to do. He closed his eyes and waited for the spectrum. It glimmered as it always did at first, like a star of light behind each eye. Then the light refracted into the many worlds. In some he saw the colours disappear and everything went black. But in some, as in shades of yellow, he made it to the top of the wall and was alive. He chose a yellow world, and letting go of the throttle, fell at speed towards the wall and Angelus.

# SEVENTEEN

ANGELUS HIT the top of the wall too quickly, his drone-copter smashing on impact. Angelus rolled into a crowd of soldiers who backed off, their pistols aimed at him.

Blake already regretted following him. What good would it do? He shifted his weight so he was facing the other side of the wall and considered gaining altitude again. But it was too late. The soldiers aimed their pistols and rifles at him. The briefcase fastened to his back, Blake continued to hurtle towards the wall. Angelus wasn't moving.

With one last thrust of power, the drone-copter dropped him on top of the wall. He deactivated it and raised both hands. 'Please. I'm a postman. Don't shoot. It was an accident. We didn't realise we'd come so far.'

'ID!' a soldier shouted, his rifle raised.

Blake pointed to the postman's badge on his lapel.

'You're a real postman?' the soldier asked with a confused expression. 'What's a postman doing out here? Why didn't your tracker warn you where you were?'

Blake held out his arm. 'It's broken.' He knew it was because of the alterations Angelus had made to it.

'They don't break,' the soldier said crossly, before pointing at Angelus. 'Who is *he*?'

'He's ... he's helping me.'

The soldier wasn't buying it. Blake was ready to reach for his pistols.

Agitated, the soldier thrust forward his rifle. 'Raise your hands and get down on your knees.'

Angelus rolled onto his front and tried to stand. He was alive!

'If I could just take a minute to explain,' Blake said, 'we'll be on our way.'

'Hands in the air!' The soldier gripped his rifle tightly.

On all fours, Angelus lifted his head. 'Why did you follow me?'

It was a mistake. And now Blake saw no way out of it.

'Wait,' Blake said to the soldier.

'Hands up!' the soldier yelled. 'On your knees.'

Blake raised his hands then slowly sank to his knees. It was over.

'I told you to keep going,' Angelus said, trying but failing to stand.

'I couldn't leave you.'

'You're an idiot.'

'You're welcome.'

'Take them downstairs.' The soldier gestured at two other soldiers.

One soldier came over and grabbed Blake's arms, wrenching them behind his back, about to use restraints. Just then a tremendous explosion from below shook the wall.

The soldier giving the orders checked his wrist. 'An attack,' he said, then pointed for the soldiers to go where he instructed them.

'Was this part of your plan?' Blake asked Angelus.

Angelus shrugged. 'Nope.'

'Stay there,' the soldier said to them before moving to peer over the wall.

Blake glanced at Angelus and indicated his collapsed drone-copter.

'You go,' Angelus whispered. 'Mine's broken.'

'We can both use this one.'

'I've told you, they're only good for one android.'

'It'll carry both of us.'

Angelus pursed his lips and shook his head. 'I'd rather take my chances with this lot.'

Blake walked closer to the edge of the wall to see who was attacking. He peered over and saw hundreds of bikes weaving across no-man's land towards the wall. Another explosion rocked the wall.

Blake and Angelus ran across the top of the wall, looking for a way down. Two soldiers tried to stop them. Blake struck one, pushing him into the other. They fell off the wall, shouting on the way down. A flurry of flames climbed the wall and took another few soldiers with it, sending them falling in balls of flame.

'Who is it?' Angelus asked.

'I don't know.'

But more and more bikes appeared, heading for the wall at speed, firing pistols and rockets.

Another explosion hit the wall, higher up. The soldiers began to return fire.

This was their chance. Blake activated his drone-copter, ran towards Angelus and grabbed him. Together, each holding one side of the drone-copter, they fell off the other side of the wall. Distracted by the attack, only one soldier opened fire on them, but missed.

'Hold on tight!' Blake shouted, trying desperately to gain altitude, but failing. The drone-copter kept falling, its propellers whining.

'I told you it would only carry one!'

Blake ignored him and twisted the throttle, giving the machine as much power as possible. The drone-copter rallied. They had made it a few hundred metres from the wall. Since the attack was happening on the other side, they were relatively safe.

They collided with the tops of trees, crashing through branches until the drone-copter got stuck and cut out completely. Blake grabbed at branches, but every time he caught one, it snapped, and he was falling again. He and Angelus crashed through branches, until finally there was the thud of Angelus colliding with the ground, swiftly followed by Blake smashing into the undergrowth. The impact knocked all the air out of his body.

He thought there was no way he would ever breathe again. His chest felt as if it had collapsed.

The colours shone more brightly than ever. The spectrum worlds: bright yellows, verdant greens, crystal blues … all of them pulsing and swirling, until Blake saw a world in which he was breathing. He chose that world. Air returned to his chest and he staggered to his feet. Angelus had managed to stand too, although he looked in worse condition than Blake.

As they limped away from the wall, using trees for cover, more explosions filled the dark sky. Then a ball of flame erupted from, or maybe through, the wall, throwing Blake and Angelus off their feet. The wall was collapsing, the soldiers on top falling.

Holding up his arms and hands to protect him from the

heat, Blake saw, through the haze, bikes coming towards them. There was no way they could run now. He was done.

'Postman!' he heard someone shout.

He couldn't see through the smoke and flames.

'Who is it?'

And then the shape on the leading bike blocked out the heat and light. Blake peered at the silhouette before him. It was a man, a ponytail fluttering behind him.

# EIGHTEEN

BLAKE RUBBED the back of his head. 'What are you doing here?'

Stig's bike shone lavender, its solar-jet an unbroken stream of light purple.

'I changed my mind.'

'You changed your mind?'

'Yeah. I gave what you said some thought. And, well ... here we are.'

Blake thought for a moment. 'Your contact, in EQ ... they're dead, aren't they?'

Stig made a face as if he wanted to lie, but then changed his mind. 'Yeah, she's dead.'

'We're glad you came,' Angelus said.

Stig winced at Angelus. 'You look like shit, kid.'

Angelus stared down at his body. Alloy showed through the bloodied, gashed skin across his arms and chest. 'Yeah. I've felt better.'

More androids appeared behind Stig, including Trevor, on a huge red bike, its solar-jet also bright red.

Stig's face was serious. 'I want your word, Postman. That

when we get the data out of Fr.e.dom's servers, you give me those Bits.'

'You have my word.' Blake avoided Angelus's eyes. The money was a lie, and he had no idea how he'd get around it if they succeeded. He decided to cross that bridge when he came to it. 'I'm not interested in Bits.'

Stig eyed him suspiciously. 'I still don't get why you're doing this.'

Blake checked that the briefcase strapped to his shoulder was in one piece. 'I want to stop Fr.e.dom. Cardinal, too.'

Stig nodded knowingly. 'You want that human, huh? What's her name?'

Blake couldn't hide his embarrassment, but kept his mouth shut.

'It's okay, kid. We all have our wants and needs. Whatever charges your core, I say. You want to get it on with a human? Your call. I've heard androids say there's nothing like it.'

'We should go,' Angelus said, 'before they send more drones.'

Behind them, more explosions rocked the wall. It wouldn't be long before Fr.e.dom repaired the wall and set about hunting them down. On this side of the wall, they were out in the open and vulnerable. Blake and Angelus got on the back of a bike. There were around a hundred bikes spread out on either side, as far as Blake could see. The bikes' solar-jets shone against the ground as they swept towards Portsmouth and the Light Bridge to the Isle of Wight. Blake didn't know how well protected the bridge would be, but had anticipated it being easier to cross than the Lundun wall, since no androids ever reached this side of the wall. He peered around the android in front of him, riding the bike, and saw more explosions up ahead. Stig's androids were fighting with what looked like a Fr.e.dom division. The bike stopped and Blake got off. Angelus was soon beside him, hiding behind a large metal container.

'There,' Angelus said, pointing. 'The Light Bridge.'

A luminous white bridge rose out of the haze of drizzle hovering above the sea. The sight was otherworldly, like something from one of William Blake's visions.

The rattle of gunfire travelled through the still, humid air.

Stig arrived beside them and pointed to a row of bikes on the ground, dead androids beside them. 'Get on a bike. We're making a run for it across the bridge.'

'What about the others?' Angelus asked.

'Those who survive will follow us.' Stig shrugged. 'Or run away. Up to them.'

Blake hated having to sacrifice so many androids, but there was no time to argue. He and Angelus climbed onto bikes of their own and, along with Stig, accelerated towards the Light Bridge.

A volley of bullets crashed against the trees they passed between, until they were out in the open. The only light came from their bikes and the bridge ahead.

'Go, go!' Angelus shouted, accelerating behind Blake. His bike lurched forward and onto the bridge. Their solar-jets hummed across the glowing white surface. Glancing behind, Blake saw they were being followed. Behind, Stig's androids fired on Fr.e.dom soldiers, who also rode bikes, chasing them. Blake faced the way he was travelling, worried that, through the mist, they would see Fr.e.dom bikes heading towards them too. Still they were speeding up, Angelus beside him and Stig just ahead. The sounds of conflict were getting closer, and Blake knew it was only a matter of time before they were in the line of fire.

To the left, across the sea and above the foaming waves, the familiar red lights of drones lit up the mist. This wasn't good. A squadron of drones met them, hovered above, then followed them across the bridge. Blake fired at them, but they moved too quickly, and he couldn't let go of the handle-bars for long because of the speed at which they were riding.

'Nearly there!' Angelus shouted.

Blake weaved from side to side, hoping this would be enough to stop the drones getting a fix on him. The bike reached what he felt was close to its maximum speed. He was over the apex of the bridge and heading downhill as the bridge sank towards the coast, so he was faster than the drones. Finally, he reached land and burst through the white haze of the Light Bridge into the cover of trees. Glancing in his wing mirror, he saw that there were about a dozen bikes left, spread out, but all heading the same way. Travelling further into the Isle of Wight, the trees disappeared, until ahead was a flat and barren field except for numerous large silver boxes set in a uniform pattern in the distance.

He followed Angelus, whose bike swayed left and right, until they reached one of the large silver buildings. They stopped beside it. Angelus reached for the briefcase on Blake's back.

'Is this it?' Blake asked. 'The servers?'

The surviving androids arrived, their bikes powering down, some of them injured and falling from their bikes. Stig and Trevor appeared.

Angelus led the way along the side of the silver building.

'Yes. We need to get inside. I can set up the exchange in here.'

'Where are the servers?' Blake asked.

'Underground.' Angelus felt along the wall for some sign of weakness or an opening, but it looked like one huge seamless chrome box.

Stig took a red package from his backpack and stuck it against the wall. 'Run!' he shouted. The box began to beep and a readout counted down from twenty.

The four of them ran through the undergrowth. Blake hit the ground just as the box detonated.

Stig appeared from beneath a tree. 'Boom!'

If ever Blake thought Stig was insane, now his suspicions were confirmed.

The smoke cleared, to reveal the walls of the silver box, peeled open. Trevor, holding his gun-cannon by his side, plodded across the ground, ready to direct it and fire on anything that came out of the building.

In the distance, the sound of more drones filled the sky.

'Get inside,' Angelus told Blake.

Blake didn't need asking twice. He made it into the silver box and climbed down a set of metal stairs until he found himself in a huge, brightly lit room. In every direction, as far as he could see, lights flickered and servers whirred. The Net, the New Net, and all the androids who had uploaded permanently, surrounded him.

'Is this all of them?' Blake asked.

'The servers are everywhere on this island,' Angelus said. 'We only need to hack into one of them and download the data.'

Blake placed a hand on one of the large grey servers and felt what he imagined was the gentle flickering of ones and zeroes.

# NINETEEN

ANGELUS OPENED THE YELLOW BRIEFCASE, took out several wires and connected them to one of the servers. From above ground came the sound of combat – the rest of Stig's men were fighting off drones and, by now, Fr.e.dom soldiers.

Stig reloaded his pistols. 'How long's it gonna take, kid?'

Angelus was busy with the terminal attached to the servers.

'He said maybe an hour,' Blake said.

Trevor face-palmed himself.

'An hour?' Stig asked. 'We won't last two minutes.'

'We need longer than that,' Blake said.

Stig walked back to the stairs and told Trevor to follow him. 'This had better be worth it. For your sake.'

'It will,' Blake said. 'You'll be a hero.'

Stig laughed. 'I'm no hero, Postman.' He climbed the stairs behind Trevor.

Angelus stared at the lights inside the yellow briefcase. 'He's going to kill us when he finds out there's no money.'

'I'm hoping he doesn't last that long,' Blake said, scanning the underground bunker. 'Do you think there's another way out of here?'

Angelus checked in all directions. 'I don't know. We'd better hope not – that would mean there's another way in.'

'Guess so.'

The readout signalled nineteen per cent.

'Nineteen per cent of what exactly?' Blake asked.

'The androids' data, uploaded.'

Blake watched the counter creep along. An explosion rocked the bunker.

'It needs to move faster,' Blake said.

'There's nothing I can do about that. It's not the quantum drive; it's these servers that are slowing down the transfer.'

The next explosion was closer. Angelus flinched, his hands shaking. 'Can you use the many worlds?' he asked Blake. 'Find out how many we can take with us.'

'*How many?* You mean we might have to leave some behind?'

'We won't save any if we're dead, will we? Come on, concentrate. Find out how many we can take and still make it out of here alive.'

Blake sat opposite the briefcase and closed his eyes. The sound of gunfire made him open them again.

'Shut it all out,' Angelus said. 'The way we practised.'

Blake nodded and bowed his head, again closing his eyes. He listened to the voice in his head, the one telling him to relax, to slow down. He searched for the colours, the sensation of the universe dividing. There was more gunfire, then something slammed against the roof. He let it all go and watched the colours glimmering. He imagined the digital readout. It flickered and accelerated up to one hundred per cent, then everything went black. He looked back at the spectrum. He was drawn to crimson, where the readout read eighty-one. All the other colours above that number had faded to black. So he knew there was no way they could take over eighty-one per cent, which meant leaving a million androids behind.

A thundering detonation brought him out of the spectrum worlds.

'Eighty-one!' he shouted. 'Eighty-one!'

Angelus held the wires attaching the briefcase to the servers, ready to pull them free.

The readout was on seventy-four.

The roof at the far end of the bunker came down, sending a wave of dust and grit over them.

'Are you sure?' Angelus shouted over the rumbling.

'I'm sure,' Blake shouted, his chest pounding.

'We have to go!' Stig shouted from the hole in the wall. 'There's more of them. Drone-bombers, too. They're gonna blow the whole place to hell!'

'Nearly there!' Blake shouted up to him.

'Seventy-nine,' Angelus said. 'Will that do?'

'No,' Blake snapped. 'We can save more. Wait.'

More of the roof fell in. The lights on all the servers surrounding them went out.

'Got it!' Angelus said, ripping the wires from the briefcase. 'Eighty-one!'

Blake strapped on the briefcase and followed Angelus up the stairs, just as the roof above where they had been working caved in, destroying the servers.

'Go!' Angelus shouted to Stig and Trevor, running past them towards the bikes.

Stig slapped Blake on the back. 'Like I said, Postman. You got balls, kid.'

They ran to the bikes and jumped on. Above them,

drones were moving into formation, ready to blanket-bomb the island, destroying all the servers and the Net. Blake thought about the million androids he couldn't help, but tried to focus on saving the ones they had saved on the drive strapped to his back.

The four of them rode back to the Light Bridge. In his wing mirror, Blake saw a squadron of drone-bombers following them.

'We won't outrun them,' Angelus said.

Stig and Trevor, to their right, had found a faster route and were ahead.

The Light Bridge gleamed through the mist. There were no soldiers anywhere; they were taking cover from the drone-bombers.

The bombs grew louder as the drone-bombers drew closer, their heat and blast-waves more and more forceful against Blake's back. Behind, an orange wall of fire and destruction edged closer. He twisted the throttle, but there was nothing left. Stig and Trevor had made it onto the Light Bridge and were flying across it.

Blake leaned as low as he could over the handlebars. He recalled travelling through the tunnel beneath the north wall at a similar speed.

The drones were almost above them. If one dropped one more bomb, they were goners. He waited for it to be over, to feel himself being blown off his bike, but the Light Bridge was close, getting closer, and he was going to make it. The front of the bike made it onto the bridge. There was no way the bombers would risk destroying the bridge, and so followed them without attacking. Blake and Angelus fired their pistols at them, grounding several of them before they backed off and flew some way across the sea either side of the bridge.

Some way ahead, the two blue solar-jets on Stig and Trevor's bikes, showed the way. Cool sea spray covered his face and turned the surface of the bridge a shade of dark graphite. He considered the weight of the quantum drive on his back. Somehow, and it made no sense to believe it was possible, the data they'd collected had made it heavier. He saw the sea, hundreds of metres beneath. The bridge was a beam of light and his luminous bike, glowing violet, was riding it.

Finally, they reached the other end of the bridge and the road into Portsmouth, heading for the wall and Lundun. The drones were no longer following them, and he expected more to meet them head-on. It was crazy to think they were going back to Lundun out of choice. But that was where Lola was. They hadn't yet worked out what they were going to do with the data, and now, since Stig was still alive, Blake had to decide what to tell him about the money he'd invented.

They rode through the early morning, hoping to find the hole Stig and his men had punched through the wall still there. In his wing mirror Blake saw, behind the gleaming Light Bridge, the Isle of Wight on fire.

Ahead, the wall was being repaired by utility-bots. Fr.e.dom had deployed a new squadron of drones, aiming to keep control and order until they had repaired the wall.

Stig and Trevor stopped, waiting for them.

'I really hate drones,' Stig said when Blake and Angelus pulled up beside him.

Trevor took something from his pocket and showed Stig.

Stig stared back at him. 'A pulse grenade? Don't you think we could have used that earlier? I don't know … maybe, when they were bombing us?'

Trevor shrugged. 'EMP grenade.'

Stig shook his head and snatched it from Trevor's huge hand. 'Sometimes, Trevor, I think you're not all there.'

Trevor's shoulders sagged. Blake felt sorry for him.

'Follow me,' Stig said, before igniting the EMP grenade and setting off at full speed towards the wall. The squadron of drones, their red lights trained on them, fell towards them.

'Launch it!' Blake shouted.

But Stig waited and waited. Finally, just as the drones opened fire, he threw the grenade. It hovered in the air, shone blue, then erupted in a beam of white light, taking out everything around it.

Weaving among the raining drones, the four of them fled through the gap in the wall, picking off utility-bots as they went.

# TWENTY

THE ANDROIDS of Lundun believed that the five million who had uploaded to the Net were gone. Blake's attack meant the destruction of the servers had happened earlier than expected. Cardinal had destroyed the Net. It was impossible to comprehend. No one believed Cardinal would go through with it. Nearly everyone spent some time on the Net, and androids believed Fr.e.dom needed it as much as, if not more than, they did.

They were wrong.

Stig had left with Trevor, intent on returning soon for the money Blake and Angelus had promised him.

Blake sat at a table opposite Angelus in an apartment in Stella Zone, WQ. They stared at the yellow briefcase and quantum drive on the table between them. If Blake could tell the androids of Lundun what they had done, maybe they would side with him and keep fighting against Fr.e.-dom. But there was no way for him to do that.

'What now?' Blake asked.

Angelus leaned forward in his chair, his eyes on the briefcase. 'There are four million androids in that thing.'

'But now there's no Net, what do we do with them?' Blake recalled Wan's gold boxes. Each one had held the CPU of an android Wan had terminated. Blake hoped the androids inside the quantum drive were oblivious to what was happening to them. As they hadn't copied the Net, or any platform in which the androids could exist, he told himself that this wasn't like Wan's boxes. But the responsibility of possessing a box that contained millions of consciousnesses made him nervous.

Blake's tracker buzzed.

Angelus stood and walked around the table. 'Is it Turing?'

On his wrist flashed up more co-ordinates. This time in Sky Zone, SQ. The sender was hidden.

'It has to be Turing,' Blake said. 'It has to be.'

'He's on the Net. How would he know?'

'I think Turing knows more than he's letting on.'

Angelus grabbed the yellow briefcase and backed away from the table. 'Let's go.'

Blake took his pistols and jacket and followed Angelus out of the apartment and down to the bikes. It struck him that he might be minutes away from seeing Lola again. The only way he'd coped with everything so far was by not thinking about her. But now he allowed himself to recall her eyes, her hair, her lips.

They crossed the border into Sky Zone. The closer they got to the co-ordinates, the more apprehensive he became. He had no idea what would be waiting for them. But they had no choice. What would they do with the quantum drive and all those androids? How else would they find Lola?

Sky Zone was much like Gold Zone, home to most of Fr.e.dom's employees. There was unrest here, as in the rest of Lundun, but not in the same way. Here, many of the androids longed for Fr.e.dom to regain control, give them back their jobs, their purpose. Now there was no Net either, a sensation of latent surrender filled the air like Lundun drizzle.

The co-ordinates took them to a bar called Serenity. They pulled up outside, checking for signs they were being watched or followed. Blake lifted his hood, swung the briefcase around to his back, and walked to the door of the bar.

'Watch your back,' he said to Angelus.

Blake pushed open the doors wondering whether Turing would be there. Maybe he would look different in reality, to preserve his anonymity. It would be unusual, but if anyone could do something like that, it would be him.

At the end of the bar was a stage, upon which a woman played blues guitar. Blake touched the briefcase strapped to his back and headed for the bar.

'Two Grits,' he said to the barman, who poured the drinks without a word and pushed them across the bar.

Angelus took one and downed it.

Blake watched him, then did the same. He was used to making deliveries like this, but he knew how quickly things could turn nasty. He asked for two more Grits and waited for the barman to meet his eyes.

'We're looking for someone who gave us these co-ordinates.'

'We're all looking for someone,' the barman said.

Blake wasn't sure what name to use, so he took the briefcase from his back and placed it on the bar. 'We have something for him.'

The barman, biting the inside of his cheek, stared at the briefcase. 'It's in there?'

Relieved the barman knew why they were there, Blake nodded. 'Is he here?'

The barman glanced at Angelus, then at the briefcase again. 'Wait here.' He walked along the bar and into a back room.

The woman playing the blues guitar finished the song and bowed at several people who were applauding slowly. She put down the guitar and walked towards Blake. She was short, pretty, with long pink hair and a flowery yellow dress that fell to the floor.

'You like the blues?' she asked.

Blake shrugged. 'Sure.'

'What's in the briefcase?'

'Nothing exciting.'

The woman faced the bar, as though ready to order. 'So, not five million androids.'

Angelus reached for the case.

'Is he here?' Blake asked.

'Follow me.' She sauntered towards the stage.

They watched her step up onto the stage and open a door that led backstage. She waited for them.

'Is this what being a postman is like?' Angelus asked.

'You know what? It's exactly what it's like.'

They followed the woman through a door and descended a flight of stairs. At the bottom was another door, illuminated by a green safety light. The woman pushed open the door, to the sound of more blues guitar.

'I don't like this,' Blake said.

'Use the spectrum.'

He tried, but all he saw was dark figures he couldn't make out, moving in the deep red lighting at the far end. He gripped the briefcase tightly then touched one of his pistols inside his pocket.

The music stopped. A figure, swamped in red light,

walked towards them. He hoped it was Turing, ready to hand over Lola.

'Postman,' a voice said. It was a voice he recognised.

'Fuck,' Angelus said, confirming Blake's thoughts. 'Cardinal.'

# TWENTY-ONE

BLAKE SNAPPED out his pistol but didn't shoot; the familiar sound of androids doing the same around him made him think twice. He scanned the room for Turing or Lola, but it was impossible to identify anyone.

'Can I take the briefcase?' the blues guitarist asked.

'You're going to have to kill me first,' Angelus said.

Blake wasn't thinking the same, but played along.

'There's only one way out of this for you both,' Cardinal said. 'And that's for you to do exactly as I say.'

His pistol outstretched, Blake walked towards Cardinal. 'Why don't I blow your CPU clean out of your head? Then we'll take our chances.'

Cardinal glanced to the side as another Cardinal, a shadow, arrived beside him.

Blake's shoulders slumped and he lowered his pistol. For all he knew, the real Cardinal, whatever that meant, wasn't even there.

'Ariel,' Cardinal said to the woman, 'I think you can take it now.'

Blake let go of the handle and let her take the case.

'No!' Angelus said, rushing for the briefcase.

Blake stopped him. 'It's no use. He could kill us and take it anyway.' Then he whispered, 'He doesn't have the password.'

Angelus stopped struggling.

'Please,' the first Cardinal said, 'follow me.'

'How do they know what we've done?' Angelus asked, walking beside Blake.

Blake had no idea how Cardinal knew about the quantum drive.

'Where's Lola?' Blake asked Cardinal. 'Is she here?'

Cardinal glanced over his shoulder. 'All in good time.'

The blues music got louder as they walked through the long, narrow room. The red light at the far end lit up the many androids, all drinking, talking, some dancing. They seemed to be oblivious to what was happening in Lundun or to the Net.

Cardinal's shadow took them into a narrow corridor, then through into what appeared to be a kind of vestibule, inside which were three doors.

'I want you to remain calm,' Cardinal said. 'This is going to be a lot to take in. You're going to be angry, but I want you to understand that my aim is to ensure that androids are treated fairly, that they have a future, and that this future is free from human persecution.'

Cardinal opened the door to their left. They walked inside. Behind a glass window, lying on a bed, unconscious, connected to a terminal, was Turing. He was identical to the figure they'd met inside the Net: tall, bald with swirling shapes tattooed on his skull.

'What is *he* doing here?' Angelus asked.

Blake tried to work out what was happening, but it made no sense.

'We made a deal,' Cardinal said. 'I wanted you – and he wanted the Net and his disciples.'

'You planned this together all along?' Blake asked.

'To be honest,' Cardinal said, 'I didn't think you'd manage it. I helped a little – fewer soldiers, fewer drone-bombers, clearing the Light Bridge – that sort of thing.'

It all made sense. Blake felt foolish. They'd walked straight into it. No wonder it had been so – relatively – easy.

Cardinal walked up to the glass, his hands behind his back. 'He's not too smart. Turing. Intelligent, though. There's a difference. I've never seen anyone code the way he can. I don't go for all this Messiah business, of course, but still... All he wanted was his own Net, in which he could house the androids who had uploaded. That's where he is now – inside the Net, preparing it for them.' Cardinal nodded at the briefcase. 'I will have control and will be the ultimate administrator.'

'Are you going to let them live?' Angelus asked. 'Those who have uploaded?'

'For now,' Cardinal said. 'But eventually they will be punished for breaking the law. For uploading.'

'And you're using Turing too?' Blake asked. 'Why did he do this?'

Cardinal spoke with an unsettling lightness. 'In the end, people do what they have to. Turing is no different. He thinks that he and his disciples will live forever in his utopia. There was no way he could develop his New Net without my facilities.'

'So you knew about that too?'

'Of course. I wanted all those androids who want to

upload permanently to do so in one place. It makes it much easier to control.'

'And Turing doesn't know what you intend to do to them?'

'Like I said, he's not very smart.'

It surprised Blake, but he was disappointed in Turing. He'd been outwardly cynical about Turing, mocking him, but deep down, he'd believed there was something special about him – like everyone had said. But he was a liar, just like the rest of them. Turing had used Blake, and there was nothing he could do about it.

'I need the password to access the quantum drive,' Cardinal said, as though asking for a favour.

'Why would we give you that?' Angelus asked.

Without a word, Cardinal walked to the door and gestured for them to follow. They followed him into the room opposite. Blake knew she would be there before he saw her.

'Lola!' Blake placed his hands against the glass.

She lay on a bed, on her side.

'She can't see or hear you,' Cardinal said.

'What have you done to her?'

Cardinal raised one hand. 'Nothing. She's fine.'

'You've locked her away!'

'And you can set her free.'

Now, Blake didn't need to work out what Cardinal wanted. It was clear. 'You want the password in return for letting her go.'

Cardinal shrugged. 'There is no loser here. Lola goes free, Turing gets his followers, and his followers get a new home.'

'But the androids will be trapped,' Angelus said. 'They will be under your control.'

'I'm merely fulfilling my end of the deal with Turing.'

'But he doesn't know what you plan to do to them all. You're going to kill them – once you have what you want.'

Cardinal waited, then spun and walked to the door. 'There is one more room.'

Blake didn't want to leave Lola. He peered through the glass, wanting to smash it down. But it was no use trying. Even if he could somehow break it, what then?

They left the room and walked into the last one. Inside were three men in white coats, standing beside a surgical chair.

'I will have the password,' Cardinal said, his voice steely, dripping with authority. 'Whatever it takes. It may take an hour, a day, a week, a month, but eventually I will have it.'

Two of the men in white coats walked towards Angelus.

'Wait,' Blake said.

'Don't tell him,' Angelus said.

Cardinal stood, his arms crossed. 'Either you tell me the password, Postman, or Lola and Angelus die. I will get the password eventually anyway, but this way you save your friends.'

The two men held Angelus's arms.

Blake tried to stop the men holding Angelus, but it was no good. 'Why don't you just destroy the drive? You're going to kill them all in time anyway.'

'I want to teach them a lesson. When I do it, they – and other androids – must witness the price they must pay.'

'Don't tell him,' Angelus said again to Blake.

Blake hit out at one of the men holding Angelus, then someone struck him from behind, knocking him to the floor. They kicked him, this time in the stomach. The room spun.

'I'll give you time to mull it over,' Cardinal said, and left the room.

Then they shot something into Blake's neck. Everything swirled around him. The last thing Blake saw was two androids strapping Angelus to a chair.

# TWENTY-TWO

THE MOMENT HE WOKE, Blake yelled, 'Stop!'

Cardinal was there, waiting for him to come round. 'The password?'

Blake tugged against the restraints, clenching his fists so hard, his nails dug into his skin. 'Let them go.'

'I will. The password?'

Blake slammed the back of his head into the chair and pulled against the restraints across his arms, chest and legs. A digi-screen lowered from above. It was divided in two. On one side, Blake saw men and women in white coats, ready to take out Angelus's CPU. On the other side was Lola, in a room, alone.

'Now is the time to decide,' Cardinal said. 'I am not playing games. The sooner we begin hacking Angelus's CPU, the sooner I can take control of the androids inside the quantum drive. I have no intention of trying to persuade you. As for Lola...' He paused, and stared off into the distance. 'She is human. I have no sympathy for humans. She will die.'

Cardinal spoke without feeling. It unnerved Blake, and

he knew immediately that there was no room for negotiation.

Walking backwards towards the door, Cardinal sighed with what appeared to be sympathy. 'Either I leave this room now and you never see me again, or you tell me the password and we can have a discussion about what happens next. The choice is yours.'

Blake's muscles relaxed. It was no use fighting the restraints, and he could see there was no use fighting Cardinal.

'I'll tell you,' he said.

Cardinal looked surprised, but soon regained his composure. He walked towards Blake.

'But how do I know you'll let them go?'

'I will let them go as soon as it is safe to do so. In the meantime, I will not harm them. I am not a sadist, Postman. I want what you want: androids to be liberated and to flourish. The only difference between us is that I am prepared to do what it takes. You are not.'

'I don't want it to happen at the expense of humans.'

Cardinal sighed. 'Which is what I have just said. Now ... the password?'

'Do you have Lola's shadow?'

Cardinal stared at him and shook his head. 'Of course not. She is dead.'

Although he looked unmoved, Blake knew he was lying. As Blake recited the password, he heard someone else speaking. It was a low, dull voice, separate from his own being. He was giving up millions of androids, and he hated himself. He tried to reassure himself that he was doing what had to be done, but still he hated listening to the capitulation in that voice, *his* voice.

'You have done the right thing,' Cardinal said, pointing

to the screen. The men in white coats surrounding Angelus backed away. There was no sound, but Blake saw Angelus realise what he had done. Angelus shouted and raged against the restraints – maybe more at Blake than against his captives. Lola was oblivious to what was happening. He wanted the screen to remain there so he could watch her, so she could remind him what he was fighting for – the freedom to love a human.

'What will you do with the androids inside the Net?'

'Turing is designing it as we speak. They will live in a digital world, as he promised them. For now.'

'And what's in it for you, exactly?'

'Turing is designing a Net for me – for all of us. His work is exquisite. I see it as an experiment. The previous Net was a haven for hackers and for those who wished to exploit its weaknesses for their own ends. It appealed to the baser elements of our creation. I want a Net that can be controlled, that can harness the power of a unified android-kind. When we have an android state, free of humans, we will need a functioning, utilitarian, beneficial Net. Androids need to live both in the real world and within a digital world. The real world appeals to our connection to humanity – to the core processing humans gave us. Maybe in time, we can alter this. The Net will give us the opportunity to program code, to advance our ability to solve problems. We can make both realms ours. Only then will androids fulfil their true potential.'

'You can't control them,' Blake said. 'It won't work.'

Cardinal narrowed his eyes. 'It *will* work. And you will help me.'

Blake had feared this was going to happen. 'How?'

'Your ability. I have seen nothing like it. I have heard rumours and have researched the possibility, but have never met an android who can do it. Show me how you see the many worlds – the spectrum. We can use your ability for the good of all android-kind.'

Blake waited, unsure how to respond.

'Help me,' Cardinal said. 'Stop fighting me and work with me to help androids.'

'It's difficult to talk to you and believe what you're saying when I am tied to this chair.'

Cardinal nodded to one of his men, who loosened Blake's restraints. Gratefully Blake sat up, rubbing one wrist then the other. They untied his legs, and he swung them over the side of the chair.

Blake needed to bide his time if he was going to get out of this. He made no commitment, but allowed Cardinal to think he might be persuaded. The digi-screen showing Lola and Angelus had been switched off. He was in the dark.

'We can end the feud between humans and androids for good,' Cardinal said. 'You can help us.'

Again, Blake gave nothing away. He didn't trust Cardinal. He knew, the first chance he had, he would kill every human in the country – and maybe, at some point, in the world. The way he spoke about androids and the need for control and order was frightening. It would be difficult, but Blake would have to be as manipulative and cunning as Cardinal if he wanted to survive, rescue Lola, and help androids on the quantum drive, in Lundun, and across the world.

# TWENTY-THREE

CARDINAL STOOD at the foot of Blake's bed. 'I want to understand how you do it. How you see the many worlds.'

Blake watched him closely.

'Describe it for me,' Cardinal said. 'Please. I will not hurt you or your friends. This is not about that. It's more important. Your ability could change everything.'

'Do I have a choice?'

'You have asked me this before. Yes, you have a choice. I would rather we do this together.' Cardinal even appeared concerned. 'I know you have struggled with your ability. And we have reason to believe that, eventually, it will kill you. If we understand how it works, then we can help you live with it.'

Again, Blake saw that he needed to bide his time. There would be an opportunity to get out of this situation. He just needed to be patient.

'I see an array of colours,' he said. 'Like when white light is refracted into the spectrum. The colours fan out, depicting the different worlds – the different options. The most beneficial world is not always obvious but, given enough time and enough worlds, I can see which reality it's best to choose.'

Cardinal shook his head slowly, in awe. 'And in those other universes, you, me, everything else continues, but on a different path?'

Blake nodded. He'd thought the same many times. It was mind-boggling, especially when in many of those universes he saw himself hurt, even killed. In these limitless universes, he no longer existed. The number of universes in which he lived would only decrease with time, which again was a sobering thought.

Cardinal's eyes were wide. 'Remarkable, isn't it?'

Blake flexed his fingers, considering all the universes.

Moving towards the bed, Cardinal spoke gently, 'We have developed an … instrument. It is intended to replicate the heightened sense of threat you feel before you see the spectrum.' He held up his hands. 'Don't worry – it won't be a genuine threat, and it won't hurt. It's simply a way of tricking your body into believing there's danger.'

For a moment, Blake saw Cardinal as a doctor, someone who actually cared for his well-being. But Cardinal was being driven by his desire to take what he needed, nothing more.

Two androids set to work on Blake. One unfastened his robe and attached wires to his chest. The other attached wires to his head. Two monitors beside his chair, which began to recline with a faint whir, bleeped, before coloured lines pulsed along them. Cardinal sat beside Blake on a similar chair, attached to the machines with similar wires.

'What are you doing?' Blake asked.

'I want to see what you see.'

Blake hoped desperately that Cardinal wouldn't be capable of seeing what he saw – or indeed of harnessing it.

'Are you ready?' Cardinal asked.

'I don't see how this can work,' Blake said.

Cardinal nodded at the two other androids. They pressed some buttons on their terminals.

A surge of what felt like cool liquid moved through Blake's head, down the back of his neck and through his spine. It grew colder and colder until he was filled with a sense of dread. He closed his eyes and saw the first flicker of colours. He was scared, having no notion of why or how this was possible. The darkness behind his eyelids flickered and spun in a kaleidoscope of colours. Then, in time with a relentless beat, the colours vibrated, until they blended again into one bright white light.

He stood inside a white room, Cardinal opposite him.

'Where are we?' Blake asked.

Cardinal surveyed the room. 'This is a generic platform, in which we have freedom.'

'To do what?'

'Experiment.'

The walls of the room flickered and were replaced by mountain walls. Blake was clinging to a ridge, his fingers digging into crevices in the rock. A fierce, icy wind blew him sideways, making him let go of the rock. He fell and struck the rocks, time and again, until he was back where he started, clinging to the rock face. *What was happening?* He told himself it wasn't real, that it was a simulation, but the moment he focused on the rock, the rational voice in his head faded away and meant nothing. The rock face went on forever; the ground was nowhere in sight. He tried to pull himself up, but it was impossible. He glanced up at his hands, gripping the rock. Then the colours spread out and he saw the spectrum. So many greens and blues showed him falling into the swirl of mist below. But in red, he saw a way out, a way of surviving. He had to push himself to the right and jump, where he would land on a ridge that was just out of view. He followed the red world, pushed his body to the right, and leapt. He fell through the air and landed on his side, smashing into the rock. But he'd made it onto the ridge.

Then he was back in the white room with Cardinal.

'I saw it,' Cardinal said. He reached to help Blake stand.

Blake refused his help and got to his feet.

'That was remarkable,' Cardinal said. 'Truly remarkable. How long does it take you to decide which world to inhabit? Does time stop while you choose?'

Breathless and shivering with the memory of clinging to the mountain, Blake tried to collect himself. 'It happens quickly. Very quickly.'

'And you see many worlds, all in different colours and shades?'

His head throbbed. Blake wanted to leave. He held his head.

'Are you in pain?' Cardinal asked.

Blake couldn't speak, but nodded.

Then the pain stopped.

He let go of his head. 'How did ... how did you do that?'

'I told you, Postman. I can help you.'

The pain in Blake's head had disappeared completely.

Then the floor moved beneath him and he was in a river, tumbling over and over, unable to catch his breath or keep his head above water. He collided with a rock and his arm twisted strangely. A sharp pain made him cry out. He held on to the rock with his other hand. Up ahead, he heard a thundering waterfall. Once again the spectrum worlds fanned out in front of him...

# TWENTY-FOUR

AFTER EXPERIENCING numerous worlds and situations, Blake lay on the floor of the white room, breathless. 'Stop. Please.'

'We need to learn how you're doing it,' Cardinal said.

'I can't keep it up,' he said, clutching his head and grimacing. 'It hurts too much.'

A second later, the pain was gone.

'How are you doing that?' Blake asked, waves of relief spilling over him.

'Eliminating the pain is easy. Pain is yet another element an android has inherited from humans. There has to be a far more elegant way of warning ourselves not to do something. Don't you think? Such as not doing something that could be harmful in the first place. Which is where your ability comes in.'

Blake was on his hands and knees. 'No ... stop.'

'We're going to see how far we can take this,' Cardinal said.

'What do you mean?'

'I want to see further into the spectrum.'

'Further?'

'I want to see years from now ... centuries.'

Blake stood, shakily. 'No. It doesn't work like that. The spectrum is immediate. It only shows me what will happen now.'

'I don't see why. We're using artificial intelligence to peer into the future – into the many worlds that will exist over the next few days, weeks, months, maybe even hundreds of years.'

'You can't,' Blake said, horrified. 'It's wrong.' The wonder in Cardinal's eyes made Blake want to stop him right there and then, but something told him it was already too late to argue or reason with him.

'Begin,' Cardinal said. It was clear he wasn't talking to Blake.

It began with noise. Blake was on his hands and knees again. It was a relentless howl, coupled with a high-pitched screeching. He buried his head in his arms, trying to block out the sound, but it was in his head, trying to get out. He opened his mouth and screamed, but there was no sound apart from the one inside his head. Then the colours came – so bright they blinded him each time they changed. He covered his eyes but, like the sound, the colours were not external; they were inside him. Blue, yellow, red, green ... one after the other, modulating through different shades, the colours flashing, blinding him. Then the colours separated into bands, each the width of an uninterrupted horizon, glowing with an effervescence he'd never seen before. This was new and different, and it scared him. The world dripped from top to bottom, the colours taking on shapes and textures, until he was standing in a wasteland, the sharp, bright colours replaced by dark, murky ones.

The noise stopped.

A huge sun glowed orange in a hazy sky. Fires burned all around, smoke drifting from right to left. It took a moment for Blake to recognise Lundun. Its towers had fallen, one leaning on another and, in the foreground, another had collapsed completely. He shuffled to his right, choking on the warm, dusty air. There was a bridge, its middle collapsed, rubble beneath it. A stiff wind blew swirls of grit and smoke over him.

He wanted to see the spectrum, but it wasn't there. Nor was the pain he usually felt after seeing it.

This place wasn't real. He told himself, over and over, that this place wasn't real.

He walked between the fires and derelict, broken buildings. The absence of anything alive struck him suddenly. There were no androids, humans or animals. The air smelled of sulphur – hot and still, with no relief.

Next to a demolished brick outhouse lay a pile of rags. Suddenly it moved, a leg kicking out. Blake ran quickly to it and reached for the bundle. He uncovered a body. A child. She was human – a girl. Her face was dirty, bruised and bloody.

'I can help you,' he said. It was instinctive, said without knowing how it was possible.

She balked at his touch, her face screwed up in pain. He moved the other rags covering her and saw that one leg was trapped beneath a steel girder. It was no good trying to move it. Blood bubbled from her mouth.

'God is android,' she said, before choking. Her eyes closed. She was dead. He backed away from her.

*What was this place? It wasn't real ... it wasn't real ...*

In the distance, on the horizon, something was approaching. Blake stopped walking, his weight on his back foot, preparing to run. It was a small black dot, growing. He walked backwards, but the dot grew bigger until it was the size of the sun, but black, completely devoid of texture or shade. Stumbling, Blake ran, glancing over his shoulder. The circle was absorbing everything, its edges warping reality like a black hole in space. It was soundless, not even whispering as it got closer and closer.

Everything went black.

Again, the colours returned, in bands across the black sky. Sound returned too, like a physical force, and again he was submerged in another world. It was the same as the last, but the buildings had fallen differently, the fires burning in different places. On the horizon, the black hole expanded. This time he didn't run. There was no point. Instead, he stared in defiance as it grew, absorbing everything.

More worlds came and went, at first scattered in ones and zeros until they melded into real worlds, all of them wastelands, all devoid of life.

Then, having witnessed countless barren worlds, the next world was different. It had a golden sheen, like twilight in late summer. The streets were empty, the sky clear, the buildings undamaged. Something had changed. Before him was an entire world waiting for inhabitants. He was surrounded by towering buildings, burnished with silver and glass. The air was fresh, laced with something sweet-smelling.

'This is just one sector of the Net,' a voice said.

It was Turing, his hands raised in surrender.

## TWENTY-FIVE

BLAKE DIDN'T KNOW how to react, or what to say. Turing had used him and had put his friends in danger.

'Do you know what you've done?' Blake asked.

Turing stopped some way from him. 'This has been difficult.'

'*Difficult? This has been difficult?*' Blake clenched his fists.

'I have learned many things,' Turing said. 'And the longer I live, the more I learn.' He moved his suit jacket and pushed his hands into the pockets of clean, pressed trousers. 'I am truly sorry I used you in that way.'

'Did you know what you were doing when we came to see you?'

He nodded. 'I did. I'm sorry. But we have little time.'

'What?'

'I have given us time alone. To talk.'

'Alone? Away from Cardinal?'

'It won't last long. I don't want to cause suspicion.' Turing moved closer and stared into Blake's eyes. 'I've made sacrifices for the ultimate good. You must believe that. I'm sure you've had to do the same. And if you haven't yet, you will soon. Believe me. There are many tough choices ahead.'

'Cardinal's using you. You have to see that! As soon as he has what he wants, he will destroy your Net and everyone in it.'

'I know what Cardinal is capable of.'

'So why are you doing this?'

Turing raised his chin. 'So that androids will have a home of their own. A truly digital world.'

'But Cardinal will destroy it.'

'I asked you,' Turing continued, 'to have faith.'

'You betrayed us.'

'You will see, in time, that I have helped you.' Turing waited, then offered his hand.

Blake stared at it. 'You sound crazy!'

'Have faith,' Turing said again, his hand still outstretched.

Blake refused the hand, but then Turing took his anyway, his grip strengthening. The colours appeared again. The spectrum fanned out, but this time it felt different – as if it wasn't just himself carrying the burden. It was Turing too. They were both doing it. They were both seeing the spectrum.

In chrome yellow, Blake saw himself holding Lola. They were together, in front of what appeared to be a door, but high up, as if they were floating, the sky behind them, a breeze moving their hair and clothes. He felt her against his chest, in his arms. Her hair smelled sweet; her hands stroked his back. They moved apart slightly and he bent down to kiss her. They kissed, and her lips were soft and her hands held the back of his head. He fell into the sensations, letting them drown him, oblivious to where he really was.

But it had to end.

His first notion was that it was a trick – that Turing, maybe even Cardinal, was tricking him.

'I see it too,' Turing said. 'The spectrum. The many worlds.'

Blake knew he was telling the truth. He'd felt it. He stared at Turing, taking it in.

'Does Cardinal know?'

'No. And we must keep it that way. If we have any chance of saving the androids you rescued.' Turing looked all around, clearly wary of their time running out. 'There is another one. Like you. Like us. You must find him. He can help you.'

Blake's mind raced. *So he was not alone!* Someone could help him understand how to use his ability without it killing him.

Again, Turing scanned all around nervously. 'I needed you to retrieve the androids from the servers. But I also needed Cardinal's facilities to design the New Net. But it has all come together, as I'd hoped. Now, the quantum drive contains everything we need for it to be self-sustainable.'

'How?'

'All that matters is that you take the quantum drive and keep it away from Cardinal and Fr.e.dom.'

'You're not making sense. I'm trapped here. And even if I could get out, there's no way I can hide the drive from Cardinal indefinitely.'

Turing exhaled and nodded sympathetically. 'I can't help you with how to keep the drive and the New Net from Cardinal. That will be up to you. But I can help you escape.'

'How?'

'It will be clear when it happens.'

'Where is the quantum drive?'

'It's inside the same room as my body, connected to Cardinal's network. He has allowed me access to it in order to work on the New Net.'

'The vision...' Blake said. 'Of me with Lola. What does it mean?'

Turing sighed. 'I'm sorry. I don't know. My visions stop at a certain point.'

'Why?'

'I'm not sure.'

Blake stared at Turing, not knowing what to say.

'What is the last thing you see?' Blake asked.

Turing swallowed and pushed back his shoulders as if in defiance. 'I see a video camera, filming me, zooming in on my face. There are no colours – no spectrum, no other worlds – just the absence of colour. Just black. No more visions or worlds.'

It struck Blake that, in the future, like Turing, there would be no colours remaining for himself – only black. At some point, there would be no lives left in any world or reality.

Turing's eyes softened. 'They hurt, don't they? The visions?'

Blake nodded.

'Malachi can help you.'

'Who?'

Turing looked around nervously. 'Head north, to Scotland. The Highlands. You will find him there. I am afraid to tell you where exactly in case Cardinal finds out. But if you travel north and use the spectrum, you will find him.'

'Who is he?' Blake asked, desperate to understand.

Turing's eyes shone with what appeared to be sympathy for him. 'I am on your side, Blake. You know that, don't you?'

'Then explain it all to me, because I feel lost, running to keep up.'

With a heavy sigh, Turing nodded. 'Very well. But we don't have much time.'

# TWENTY-SIX

A GUST of warm air swept by them. Blake waited eagerly for Turing to give him answers to the questions he'd had for so long.

'I was first-generation android, and one of the first coders who designed the second generation of androids. It all happened so quickly. We were following the science, day after day, hour after hour, the results accelerating. It was a heady time – everything seemed possible. There is no fundamental difference between androids designed by humans and those designed and built by androids. There are subtle differences to the mechanics, sure, but as for computation, or intelligence, we had to remain within the constraints issued by humans.'

Blake suspected that Turing wasn't telling him every-thing. 'But you improved on the computation, didn't you?'

Turing stared out towards the horizon, which glimmered and shone yellow.

'It happened so fast,' Turing said. 'The two of us, Malachi and I, followed the coding in other directions. We couldn't stop.'

'What happened?'

'The company we worked for in Gold Zone, a subsidiary of Fr.e.dom, grew suspicious of our coding and our work, so we left. We were scared for our lives, so we hid.'

'What did you find with your coding? Why were they suspicious?'

Turing met his eyes. 'We discovered the spectrum.'

Blake waited for it all to make sense, to come together in his mind, but there was still something missing.

'So *you* created it?' Blake asked. 'You designed the spectrum?'

Slowly, Turing nodded. '*We* did. Malachi and I. It was a theoretical idea that had been growing in popularity for some time, but the more we worked on the next generation of android, the more we began to see it was possible. When we heard rumours that Fr.e.dom was asking about our work, we knew we were on to something – and, in the wrong hands, it could cause massive problems.'

'Where do I come into all this? Why me? Why do I see the spectrum?'

Turing stroked his chin. 'I ... *we* designed you.'

Blake's mind clouded with confusion. 'No. I was made by Blood and Bone. I was a shadow.'

'Yes,' Turing said.

'You worked for Blood and Bone?'

Turing exhaled noisily. 'Yes... I didn't know what they planned to do with you, or the others. If I'd known, I would never have helped them.'

'What did you think a human terrorist group was going to do?'

'I didn't know that's what they were. They contacted us, helped us escape from Lundun, then gave us the facilities and materials we needed to continue our work.'

'That's when you travelled north? To Scotland?'

Turing nodded. 'We were obsessed. We wanted to develop our understanding of quantum mechanics and the many worlds theory.'

'How many of us are there? How many androids can use the spectrum?'

'They asked us to develop six shadows.'

'Six? Did you ask why they wanted them?'

Turing rubbed the back of his neck and shrugged. 'We were more concerned with whether we *could* do it rather than whether we *should*.'

'Where does the spectrum come into this? Did Blood and Bone know about it?'

'Yes. That's why they were helping us – they provided us with the means to create the android shadows. But we weren't convinced it would work. Or if it did, without experimenting, we didn't know what an android with that capability would be able to achieve. We were concerned that it might give the android powers and abilities far beyond any living human or android. The fact that these androids would be shadows, controlled by humans, gave us some reassurance that we weren't creating destructive monsters.'

'You said you can see the spectrum as well. How?'

'To ensure what we were doing was ethical, we experimented on ourselves.'

Blake was still working to take it all in. It still seemed crazy that all this had happened, and that he was an integral part of it.

'It required the two of us,' Turing continued. 'I was first. Malachi reprogrammed my CPU. I was scared it would change me – that I wouldn't be me any longer. When I woke from the procedure, the world looked different. It was impossible to describe, but it was different. I was different...'

'And you could see the spectrum.'

'Yes. We carried out many experiments. When we were under stress, and the fight-or-flight mechanism was activated, the spectrum began to appear. It was disorientating, and took some time to grow accustomed to it. But when I did, after some practice, I began to take control. That's when the pain started.'

'Pain? In your head? After seeing the spectrum?'

Turing nodded. 'It is a side effect. A very unwelcome one.'

'So how did you stop it?'

'I haven't. I have to limit how often I use the spectrum. I have learned over time how to reduce the pain I feel, but it's always there.'

'What about Malachi? He can see it too?'

'He was next. I carried out the procedure on him, aiming to make improvements on what he had done to my CPU.'

'Did it work?'

'Yes, but the pain was still there. We couldn't eradicate it.'

Blake took a moment to think. Now he knew where he'd come from, the past no longer seemed so distant, or indistinct. This gave him solace – something he hadn't realised he was searching for.

'Malachi changed his mind. He didn't want to use the spectrum with the shadows Blood and Bone had asked us to develop.'

'But *you* did?'

Turing pursed his lips, his eyes filled with regret. 'I was foolish. I see that now. But I wanted to help create the next generation of androids. A generation of androids that would give us a new future. If they could read the future, predict the best path for all of us, it would only lead to good things.

But it doesn't work that way. The spectrum allows an android to see which reality is best for them, not for all androids. And what is beneficial for one may not be so for all.'

Blake didn't know what to say. Part of him wanted to agree with Turing – to tell him he understood.

'Malachi left without another word. That was nearly ten years ago. But I know he's still out there. In Scotland. The Highlands. He can help you understand the spectrum. And he can help you with the pain. I know he will have been working on it, learning all this time.'

'So why the New Net? And the Messiah?' Blake asked. 'Where did that come from?'

'I had no intention of being known as the Messiah. Only a crazy person would.'

'So how did it happen?'

'I have no idea. Other androids came to me, asking if they could work on the New Net. It grew and grew until there were hundreds and thousands of androids uploading.'

'But you must have seen how wrong it was.'

'Why? Many of these androids were living in squalor. I saw no reason why they should live that way. I was giving them a way out.'

'But it isn't real. The Net. Your New Net – it's not real.'

'Why?' Turing asked. 'Why isn't it real?'

Blake could think of no better reason than to repeat himself. 'Because it isn't real. Lundun, Earth – that's real.' He raised his hands. 'All this is just ... ones and zeros. Nothing else.'

'We have the chance of giving millions of androids a home – a good life. I don't understand why you or anyone else can't see that.'

Blake shook his head slowly.

Turing faced the sky. 'Cardinal will bring you out of it soon.' He reached for Blake's arm and held it. 'When Cardinal discovered what I was doing, he demanded that I help find you. That's how we ended up here. He wants to understand how the spectrum works. But I knew, all along, that you and I could work together to save all those androids.'

'He has Lola's shadow, doesn't he?'

Turing nodded. 'He believes that Lola's shadow will help him understand the spectrum so he can use it himself. I don't know if he will succeed. Cardinal thinks you are the only android who can see the spectrum. We can't let him learn how to use it.'

'What do I do?'

'You will know when to escape. Take the quantum drive with you. Keep it from Cardinal.'

'How?'

Turing interlocked his fingers. 'I don't know. But you must. I will do all I can to help you and Lola's shadow.'

'I don't know how I can keep the drive hidden from Cardinal.'

'We're out of time. For now, have faith.'

'But ...'

Blake awoke, gasping for air.

'We had to bring you back,' Cardinal said. 'We had no way of tracking where you were.' Cardinal looked suspiciously at him, before instructing the androids in white coats to try again.

Blake was convinced Cardinal had no idea where he'd been, or that he'd spoken to Turing. For the first time in a long time, he saw a future – not just for him, but for humans and androids. He went back into the worlds Cardinal had made for him, repeatedly. Finally, he was so tired, he couldn't be sure the room he was in was real or not. He didn't care. The worlds had stopped and he had been still for around a minute. His head throbbing, his mouth dry and his body aching, he rolled onto his side. There must have been at least a hundred worlds and each was almost identical – a wasteland, filled with destruction and dead bodies. That was what Cardinal wanted. He wanted to see a future in which only androids survived. But there was no sign of androids in that place either. Blake recalled the dead humans he'd found, especially the small girl, who he'd seen several times. She said the same thing each time before she died, and every time it made him cold. 'God is android.'

# TWENTY-SEVEN

CARDINAL MADE Blake spend what felt like days searching for a reality in which androids existed and were alive and flourishing. But each world he saw was barren, destroyed, devoid of life. Some realities appeared more hospitable to life than others, with vegetation, the occasional bird. But these worlds were few and showed no signs of intelligent life, human or android.

He focused on slowing his breathing, guarding himself from the pain that came with experiencing the spectrum. Cardinal entered the room.

Blake couldn't get used to the way he felt when he was near Cardinal, who exuded a certainty that Blake could not fathom. Cardinal was always sure – about everything. Blake wondered how it was possible. It was as though he had already lived several lives, gaining knowledge and experience as he did so, until he was the complete android Blake saw before him.

Cardinal spoke with his usual poise. 'It is time to vanquish the dogma surrounding androids.'

'Dogma?' Blake asked.

Cardinal nodded slowly. 'From the very beginning, because androids operate digitally, humans viewed us as being incapable of attaining certain states of being. Because humans created androids, they assumed that we should be subservient to them. I don't believe this follows.'

Blake agreed, but he didn't say anything.

Cardinal continued, 'Humans insist that androids are incapable of free will. When they create an android, humans issue it with a base code, allowing the android to learn. Because they give this initial coding to the android, any subsequent learning is governed by, and influenced by, it. Therefore, androids have no free will. But this is no different to a human and their genetic material. A human has no choice in their heritage, any more than an android has input into their base coding. Neither, if we take this premise, has free will. Humans and androids are determined by their initial conditions and environment. Our genetics are determined. But androids, just like humans, try to bend determinism to its limits.'

Listening to his argument, Blake found nothing to disagree with. What Cardinal said, Blake also believed.

'And then there is love,' Cardinal said, his eyes fierce.

Blake wanted to look away, but couldn't.

'Androids feel love too,' Cardinal said. 'Do you agree?'

Blake nodded.

Defiance flashed across Cardinal's features. 'I have loved. I know what it means to love.'

Blake spoke slowly. 'How do you know what humans feel as love is the way androids feel when they claim to be in love?'

Without hesitation, Cardinal replied. 'I don't. But how do you know that all humans experience love in the same way? How do they know what another human feels when they claim to be in love?'

That was true, but it didn't get to the heart of what Blake was asking.

'Do *you* think it is different?' Cardinal asked.

Blake considered his answer. 'No.'

Cardinal looked relieved not to have to argue his point. Blake waited as Cardinal tilted his head.

'I've seen the way you look at her,' Cardinal said.

'Who?' Blake asked, playing dumb.

Cardinal's gaze met Blake's. His serious expression told him there was no time to play the fool.

'Once, I was in love with a human,' Cardinal said.

Blake didn't know what to say.

'You remember I was a soldier? When I escaped from my captors in Russia, a young woman took me in. Her name was Zoya. I was close to death when she found me. She told me, when I was well enough, that she hated what humans had done to androids. She had never met an android. My eyes fascinated her – she'd never seen an android's yellow eyes before. She hid me away from her family, in a barn on her father's farm. Being there was like travelling back in time, before cities, before Lundun. Each night, she stayed with me. She agreed to leave with me when I had recovered enough. But the night before we planned to leave, her father found us in the barn. He'd grown suspicious when food, drink and some of his clothes had gone missing. He woke us, standing there, aiming a shotgun at me. He was furious, demanded that I leave at once. I had no choice. Zoya clung to me, begging me to take her too, but her father would have killed us both if I had. I was forced to leave her there. As I walked through the frozen forests, I convinced myself it was hopeless – that I could never give Zoya the life she deserved.

They would never allow us to be together. By the time I'd come to my senses, I'd walked miles, and it was too late. I convinced myself I was doing the right thing, and kept on going west towards Lundun and home. Even then, I saw Lundun as my home. I was foolish.'

Blake stared at Cardinal, trying to work out if he was telling the truth. But everything about him told Blake he was.

'I know how you feel,' Cardinal said. 'You are wondering whether you are good enough for her. You are questioning whether she sees you the same way she sees human men.'

'Does she?' Blake asked without thinking.

Cardinal pursed his lips in sympathy. 'Who knows?' He stroked his chin in thought. 'But then, can you ever be sure that the person you love feels the same way you do? Isn't this the root of all insecurities that lead to jealousy or possessiveness? I know I have experienced them.'

Blake had too, and wanted to tell Cardinal so. 'But you want to kill humans,' he said. 'Why do you want to kill humans if they're the same as us?'

'I didn't say they were the same.'

And here was the point at which Blake and Cardinal parted ways.

'I don't see how, if what you say is true, you see them as different.'

Cardinal raised an eyebrow, as though he'd bested him in a game of chess. 'I know. Which is why they, and most likely she, will be your downfall.'

# TWENTY-EIGHT

YET AGAIN, Blake was dragged out of the spectrum, leaving him breathless and disorientated. It took him several minutes to recover. His vision was blurred, his head pounding.

'It's there,' someone said. 'I don't believe it. It's right there.'

Blake wiped his eyes and tried to focus on the figures beside his chair. He focused on a face, their eyes wide with wonder.

'We've done it,' another voice said.

Blake's vision was returning, the edges of shape and colour working into some kind of order. Two androids in white coats stared at a large digi-screen. On it was what looked like an equation, or a list of code.

It made no sense to Blake. 'What ... is it?'

One android looked at Blake, clearly unsure how to respond.

Cardinal hurried into the room. 'What is it?' he asked again.

'Cardinal,' the android said, his voice urgent. 'We did it.'

'Is that it?' Cardinal asked, pointing to the digi-screen. 'You've mapped the spectrum?'

The two androids in white coats glanced at one another. 'Yes,' the taller one said. 'We think so.'

Cardinal stared at the digi-screen, then glanced at Blake. 'You have helped us. More than you can know.'

'What do you mean?' Blake asked, trying to sit up.

Cardinal pointed to the digi-screen. 'Look. Isn't it beautiful?'

The coding Blake saw made no sense to him. 'What … is it?'

'It is the spectrum,' Cardinal said, transfixed. 'It has taken time and effort, but we have isolated the coding inside you that is different to the coding in other androids. It is a subtle difference, but it unlocks the spectrum. It is quite remarkable that this coding can do something so miraculous.'

Blake read the code. They had taken it straight from his CPU. He felt violated and had no words.

'How long before we can use it?' Cardinal asked, an excitement in his voice that Blake had not heard before.

Neither android in white coats answered.

'How long?' Cardinal asked again.

'We're not sure,' one of them said.

Cardinal edged closer to the digi-screen. 'But it can be done? We can use it?'

Blake waited, as eager as Cardinal to hear their response.

'Again, we can't be sure. We have just drawn the coding from the patient. There is still a great deal of work to do.'

'You can't do this,' Blake said. It was a childish thing to say, but he felt possessive. It was *his* ability.

'It is done,' Cardinal said without feeling. He turned to

leave, speaking to the two androids as he walked towards the door. 'I want you working on this around the clock. Do whatever you need to do. Use as many androids as you have to. I want the spectrum as soon as possible.'

Everything inside Blake yelled at him to go after Cardinal, to end it all now and kill him, but he could barely focus, never mind take on Cardinal. He tried to move from the chair.

'Please,' one android said, laying a hand on his shoulder. 'Stay where you are. You shouldn't move yet.'

'Let me go,' Blake demanded.

Then he felt the sensation of falling again, and a cold liquid moving through his veins. It was no use fighting.

## TWENTY-NINE

BLAKE LAY on his back in bed, in the dark. He'd trained himself over the years not to power down so much that he lost awareness. A few moments each day to defragment was all he needed. He used these quiet times to think. And that was exactly what he was doing when the lights went out.

He sat up, and made out an unfamiliar sound, something he'd not heard in that place before: shouting in the distance. And gunfire. Then the shouting grew louder. Something was moving outside, just above him. Drones, maybe. An explosion rocked the building, followed by two more. The power came back on, then went off again. This time, the doors to his room opened. He stared at the swinging doors for a second before leaping out of bed to stop it closing. In the corridor he met Angelus, who was running, opening each door he came to and checking inside.

'What's happening?' Blake shouted.

'No idea!' Angelus shouted. 'But let's get out and ask questions later.'

'We have to find Lola.'

Blake recalled what Turing had said about helping them escape. He tried several rooms but was unable to find her. He hoped Angelus was having better luck. In one room he found pistols and ammunition, so he loaded up with as much as he could carry. Finally, after trying three more rooms, he returned to the main corridor to see Lola stumble out of a room and into Angelus's arms.

She was okay. Blake wanted to hold her right there and then, the way he'd seen in his vision.

'We have to go,' Angelus said, supporting Lola.

'Not yet,' Blake said. 'We need the quantum drive.'

'Why?'

'Trust me. We need to take it with us.' He remembered where Turing's room was, and opened the door. Turing lay on a bed, unconscious, hooked up to a terminal.

Angelus took out his pistol and aimed it at Turing.

'Stop!' Blake shouted. 'Don't.'

'He betrayed us,' Angelus shouted. 'He's the reason we're in this mess!'

'Just wait,' Blake said.

Lola was pulling Angelus away. 'We don't have time for this. We should go. Now!'

'I can't leave him here alive,' Angelus said. 'Not after what he's done. All those androids who followed him...'

'Trust me,' Blake said, searching the room for the quantum drive. 'It's not what you think.'

'He tricked them. All of them,' Angelus said.

Blake found the drive in the far corner of the room, hooked up to a terminal. He unhooked it carefully and cradled it. The drive glowed a fluorescent blue.

'What is that?' Lola asked.

'It's a quantum drive. Contains all the data that androids

need. The New Net, along with every android who uploaded, is in here.'

Angelus stared at Turing, his pistol outstretched.

Blake spoke slowly. 'Put the gun down.' He glanced around, looking for cameras and recording equipment. He couldn't risk telling Angelus what had happened in his vision, in case Cardinal found out.

'He lied to them … lied to us. He used us and helped Cardinal trap millions of androids. We have to stop him. He's helping Cardinal.'

Angelus looked determined.

'I don't have time to explain,' Blake said.

Angelus tightened his grip on the pistol.

'He said we have to trust him,' Blake said. 'That we must have faith. Remember?'

Angelus laughed cynically and moved even closer to the bed. 'Faith? You're as crazy as he is. We can't trust him.'

Blake took out his pistol and aimed it at Angelus. 'We have to.'

'What are you doing?' Lola asked Blake, panic in her voice.

Angelus glanced over at him. 'You've lost your mind. What has Cardinal done to you?'

Blake spoke as calmly as he could. 'Drop the pistol, Angelus. Please.'

Angelus focused again on Turing. 'I'm not leaving until he's dead.'

'He said I'd have to make tough choices. He said we have to think of the ultimate good. Don't you see? It's Turing who is doing this – he has turned off the power. He told me I would know when to escape. He told me where to find the quantum drive.'

'He's letting Cardinal control millions of androids in a digital prison before killing them all!'

'That won't happen. Lower the pistol.'

'Please,' Lola said, a palm raised to each of them. 'Stop. We have to go before Cardinal's soldiers get here.'

'He's doing this ... helping us escape,' Blake said, pointing at Turing. 'If you kill him, Cardinal will find us and take back the quantum drive. I can't let you do that.'

Angelus spoke through gritted teeth. 'They've brainwashed you.'

Maybe they had, but Blake knew he had to stop Angelus from killing Turing.

For five seconds, no one said anything. Angelus pointed his pistol at Turing and Blake pointed his at Angelus.

Then what felt like an earthquake shook the walls of the building, making the three of them drop to the floor. Dust filled the room. Through the dust, the spectrum unfurled in front of Blake. It happened so quickly: the blues and yellows, switching to reds. Blake looked for a world in which they escaped. Time and again, he saw Angelus shoot and kill Turing. Repeatedly, the power returned, or drones swooped down from the sky. In each world, Fr.e.dom soldiers caught them. The only world in which he saw them escaping was purple. But in this world, he had to shoot Angelus. It was the only way.

But he couldn't do it. There had to be another way.

Shouting and gunfire came from along the corridor.

Dazed, Blake got to his feet. Angelus was already standing, his pistol trained on Turing again.

'No!' Blake shouted. 'You can't kill him. We need him. Trust me!'

An explosion above sent chunks of concrete falling from the ceiling.

'I'm sorry,' Angelus said.

Blake had no choice. He shot Angelus in the chest.

Lola ran over to Angelus, who lay on the floor. 'What have you done?' she shouted. 'Why did you do that?'

Blake, his pistol still outstretched, felt a chill run through him. His feet were unable to move. *What had he done?* He told himself he'd had to do it. The lights on the terminal beside Turing's body shone red: alerts asking for medical assistance due to the power outage.

Then someone knocked into him from behind. It was too late. It had to be Fr.e.dom soldiers.

'Someone owes me twenty thousand Bits,' a voice said. It was Stig, followed by Trevor.

'Help me!' Lola shouted, beckoning Trevor over.

'What's going on here then, kid?' Stig asked, nodding over to Angelus. 'He dead?'

'No,' Blake said. 'I don't think so.'

Trevor grabbed Angelus as if he was a doll, slung him over one shoulder and walked out of the room. Lola followed him, glaring at Blake.

'What did you do?' Stig asked, smirking. 'She's pissed at you, kid.'

'I shot him,' he said.

'*You* did? Well, I'll remember to watch my back.' Stig pulled Blake's arm. 'Let's go.'

Blake looked at Turing one last time, hoping he'd done the right thing. Then the sensation that he'd been tricked came over him. He wasn't sure of anything now.

'Is that what I think it is?' Stig asked, pointing to the quantum drive. 'Are they all in there? The androids?'

Blake nodded.

The wall and roof of the corridor outside the room had been peeled away. They climbed up over the rubble.

Outside was a self-driver. They got inside, Angelus lying against Lola.

Trevor took control of the car, did a U-turn, then accelerated between squat brick buildings, up a hill and onto an open road.

'Where are we?' Blake asked.

'Sky Zone,' Stig said. 'This place is pretty hidden away.'

Blake looked out of the window at the apartment towers of Sky Zone only a few blocks away.

Lola opened Angelus's jacket and examined the bullet wound.

'Let me help,' Blake said.

'Don't!' she snapped. 'Don't touch him.'

'I had to,' he said. 'You don't understand—'

'Leave it,' she said. 'You have no idea what this man has done for your kind. And you shot him.'

'I'm sorry.'

'You'd better hope it hasn't damaged his core.'

Stig leaned over from the passenger seat. 'We got a message, saying when and where to attack. I didn't think much of it, but we turned up to see for ourselves. Then, as we were about to leave, the power went out and drones started falling out of the sky. The easiest rescue you could think of.'

Turing must have been behind it.

'I know where to take him,' Blake said, glancing over at Angelus. He told Stig the co-ordinates.

# THIRTY

'WHY AMBER ZONE?' Stig asked.

'Angelus has a friend there who can help repair him and keep him hidden.' Blake rested the quantum drive on his lap. Now it was disconnected, it no longer shone with a blue light. He hoped it hadn't been damaged in their escape.

Lola still wouldn't look at him. The thought that she didn't trust him, or that he was a traitor, cut him deeply.

'It will all make sense,' he said to her. 'I promise.'

She ignored him.

Angelus hadn't moved since Blake had shot him. Blake hoped someone could repair the damage. Androids were more than just their CPU. Many experiments had shown that CPU transplantation did not replicate the individual. Androids, like humans, were a combination of body and mind.

'Cardinal has got to you.' Lola stared at the quantum drive on Blake's lap. 'What lies did he tell you to make you do that?'

'It wasn't Cardinal,' he said. 'It was Turing. I met him alone, in the Net.'

'But he wasn't alone. Don't you see? It's all a trick. He tricked you so you'd end up in that place, and he's making a fool of you again.'

'But we've escaped. And we have the drive.'

'I don't know how or why, but this must be part of Cardinal's plan too.'

'No. I don't believe that. The way Turing spoke ... it was—'

'Was what? They call him the Messiah because he's good at what he does. He manipulates people for his own ends. Why can't you see that?'

Blake felt stupid. The idea that he had been tricked came back to him again. Turing had done it once before – what if he'd done it again? But why would Cardinal want them to escape like that? No, it had to be Turing helping them.

'How do we know this isn't a trap?' Lola asked. 'Taking us to Amber Zone?'

'It's not a trap. Neither Cardinal or Turing has any idea where we're going. Angelus will be safe there.'

She stared at him, her eyes dark and angry. 'Safe?'

He wanted to convince her but didn't have the words. Instead, he stared out of the window the rest of the way.

They got out of the car and walked towards the front of the enormous house. Blake had put the quantum drive in his postbag, which he carried over his shoulder. He knocked on the door. Trevor's huge frame was behind him, Angelus draped over his shoulder.

The door opened. Before the man who answered had a chance to speak, Blake led the way inside.

'Excuse me,' the android said, attempting to push him back out of the door. 'Please leave.'

'Where's Francesca?' Blake asked loudly, hoping she'd hear him.

She appeared on the staircase in the lofty hallway. 'Who is it, Gerard?'

Gerard thrust his hands down by his side. 'I've asked them to leave, but they won't listen.'

Francesca stared down at them from the stairs, then ran down to them. 'Is that ... is that Angelus?' Covering her mouth, she reached up to touch Angelus's face. 'What happened?'

Lola glanced at Blake.

'He's been injured,' Blake said, ignoring Lola's stare. 'We need your help.'

'Where is he hurt?' Francesca asked. Trevor lowered Angelus to the floor. 'Gerard, get the mechanic.'

Gerard was clearly confused. 'Miss Riley?'

'The mechanic!' she shouted. 'Harry. Get Harry!'

Gerard hurried away, using his wrist to hail the mechanic.

'Has it harmed his core?' Francesca asked, reaching out to the hole in Angelus's chest.

'We don't know,' Blake said. 'I don't think so.'

Stig, his hands on his hips, scanned the massive hallway. 'This is some place you have.'

Francesca wasn't listening, instead whispering something to Angelus, brushing back his long grey hair from his face. 'Who would have done something like this?' she asked.

'I did it,' Blake said.

Francesca's hand froze, and she got to her feet. '*You* did it? Why?'

'He was ... I had to.'

'Get out,' she said, pointing to the door. 'I knew the first time I saw you that you were no good for Angelus.'

'I can explain,' he said.

'Out,' she said again. 'I will take care of him. I want you all out of my home.'

Blake thought about trying to explain, but decided it was best to leave her alone for now. There would be time for explanations later.

The door closed behind them. Stig and Trevor got into the self-driver.

'He's going to be okay,' Blake said to Lola.

'How could you shoot him?' she asked and, for the first time since he'd done it, met his eyes.

'If there was another way, I would have chosen that. I promise.'

For a moment he thought she might believe him. But her expression changed and she shook her head. 'You're wrong. Cardinal has got to you.'

He watched her get into the car. He still felt that he'd done the right thing. Not until it was all over would he be vindicated. He got into the car.

'So,' Stig said. 'Where are the Bits you owe me, kid?'

'When this is over, I promise, I'll give you double.'

'*Double?* Double of nothing is still nothing.'

Blake checked the quantum drive. 'Letting Cardinal get away with what he wants won't help you either. Work with us and I promise it'll be worth your while.'

'You know what's going to happen if you double-cross me like you did your buddy in there?'

'I didn't double-cross him.'

'Maybe you didn't shoot him in the back. But you shot him all the same.'

Trevor's hulking shoulders bounced up and down as he laughed, reaching inside his huge coat and pulling out a sandwich.

'Where are we going?' Stig asked. 'I guess I'll stick around until I get my Bits. If I don't get them, I can always hand you and that quantum whatever-it-is over to Cardinal for a sizeable reward.'

'Head for NQ,' Lola said. 'We need to get weapons and ammunition if we're going to fight off Fr.e.dom until we work out what to do with that thing.'

'You hear that, Trevor?' Stig said, punching the big guy's arm. 'You like a good fight, huh?'

Trevor grunted, wiped his nose with a fist, and took a huge bite out of his sandwich.

# THIRTY-ONE

THE NEXT MORNING, the streets were crawling with Fr.e.dom soldiers.

Lola still wasn't talking to Blake.

Stig offered Blake a bottle of Grit, having taken a swig and wiped his mouth with the back of his hand.

Blake raised an eyebrow. 'It's morning.'

Stig shrugged, screwed the lid onto the bottle and threw it across the room to Trevor, who caught it, unscrewed the lid and guzzled thirstily.

Blake leaned forward to watch the digi-screen. All morning, Fr.e.dom's military had been issuing warnings about what androids could and couldn't do in Lundun. Not only was movement between Quadrants restricted, but this had been extended to between zones. A curfew had also been enforced, preventing androids leaving their apartments after sundown without being questioned as to whether travel was essential.

'Androids won't stand for this,' Stig said.

Blake considered it for a moment. He didn't see androids fighting back. 'They don't have a choice.'

Stig sniffed loudly. 'Androids are free to do as they wish.'

'Androids have never been free.'

'I've been my own android all my life. Nothing's gonna change that.'

Blake gave up. Androids like Stig didn't have a clue. He might think he was free. But in reality, Lundun's walls were his cage. The androids had all been told that the wall existed to protect them, but Blake knew better. Stig and his sort were part of the problem – enslaving androids through the sale of Mirth. But discussing politics with Stig would be pointless.

Cardinal was due to give a statement at any minute, but Blake already knew what he was going to say. Cardinal's dream – to control Lundun – was about to come true. And Blake, inadvertently, had helped. Lola, Angelus and the others, in launching a revolution, had given Cardinal and Fr.e.dom the excuse they needed to take total control of the city. Blake hadn't seen it coming, and he felt like a fool. Cardinal would have known – that was the difference between them. Maybe all along, Cardinal had been willing for them to begin a revolution so androids would see for themselves the price they paid for not embracing state control.

On the digi-screen, Cardinal stepped up to the podium.

Blake imagined countries around the world taking note. There wasn't one country in the world that was governed by androids. But in the UK, it was about to happen. Maybe other countries would help humans in the UK – send support and assistance. There might still be time to negotiate and work out how best to move forward.

Cardinal cleared his throat, taking his time to nod at many of the androids in the room. Then he acknowledged the camera. His dark eyes glowed.

Lola came into the room to listen.

Cardinal spoke. 'This morning, android-kind wakes to a new day, a new world, a new era. For many years, humans have viewed androids as second-class citizens in Lundun, the UK and the world. No longer. No longer will humanity exploit androids.' Cardinal paused, again scanning the room, before calmly focusing on the camera. 'There will be disquiet around the world concerning what is happening in this city. But that is because humanity still runs the world. We will be the first beacon for android-kind and its desire to be treated fairly, equally and with respect. Here in Lundun, we will begin a movement that will not stop until androids around the globe are seen as equal to humans, and are valued.' Cardinal placed both hands on the podium and leaned towards the camera.

Blake hadn't realised how similar their own manifesto was to Cardinal's. But what Cardinal *wasn't* saying – about what he intended to do to humans – made all the difference.

'You have every reason to be wary of what I am about to tell you. Change of this magnitude is frightening. But you must take comfort in knowing that I, like you, am android, and want what is best for our kind.' He stood up straight and lifted his chin. 'First, I am declaring martial law. The three enclaves in the UK will be governed by the military divisions of Fr.e.dom. We have prepared for this and are ready to enforce order in every one of our quadrants and zones. Second, we will issue each android a permit that they must keep with them at all times. This entitles them to the freedom of their zone. Third, we have developed a second iteration of the Net, one that is far superior to its predecessor. There will be no more permanent uploading to the Net, and we will limit usage of the Net to those who are law-abiding citizens.'

'Does he know he doesn't have the drive?' Stig asked, pointing at the quantum drive in the postbag on the table.

Blake stared at the bag and thought how it was only a matter of time before Cardinal got his hands on it again. Unless he did something.

Cardinal's eyes softened and he tilted his head. 'We will deal with all those androids who broke the law and uploaded permanently to the Net. I can only apologise on their behalf for letting you down. I, like you, have no sympathy for those who refuse to contribute to the flourishing of android-kind.' A soft ripple of applause came from the digi-screen. 'Fourth, despite the efforts of small terrorist groups who continue to attack our infrastructure, we will, at noon today, launch a satellite designed to track the whole of the country, monitoring movement, interactions, and the threats posed to us by humanity and android traitors. This surveillance is for you ... for all of us. It will keep us all safe.'

Once the satellite was above them, Blake knew there'd be nowhere to hide.

Another burst of applause broke out before Cardinal spoke again. 'I declare Lundun to be the first android state of its kind. Lundun and the UK are only the beginning. Soon, countries and states around the world will join our android republic. Then we will unify android-kind under one flag. The android flag.' He waited a moment. 'Unfortunately, humanity has shown us on too many occasions that it cannot be trusted. And so, as of midnight tonight, we will quarantine any human found in the UK until we decide on a solution and can remove them. Androids are peaceful. We do not want war. But this does not mean we will not deal in war. We will fight to attain, and keep, our autonomous android state safe.'

The applause grew louder. Cardinal raised his hands to

the onlookers, then to the camera. 'Today is an important day – a day that we will remember for centuries. We stand together like no collection of androids has ever done before. We stand together and refuse to be ignored, objectified or persecuted any longer. The tenth of December 2118 will now and forever be known as Android Independence Day.' Cardinal left the platform to another round of applause, and the digi-screen went black.

Stig threw the empty bottle of Grit at the digi-screen, smashing both.

Blake couldn't imagine how the androids of Lundun could listen to Cardinal and side with him. They would each know someone who had uploaded to the Net. And androids didn't see those who had as traitors. But Cardinal was clever. Describing them as traitors would no doubt convince some that that was exactly what they were.

Outside, drones patrolled the skies and self-drivers manned by soldiers patrolled the streets.

# THIRTY-TWO

THE REVOLUTION BLAKE had helped to begin with Angelus and Archer was over, hijacked by one that had been designed on a much larger scale, by an individual with the weight of Fr.e.dom behind him. Unlike their revolution, which had been based on the notion of androids and humans living side by side, Cardinal's revolution promoted no such camaraderie. He wanted the opposite. He wanted division.

Lola still hadn't spoken to Blake since he'd shot Angelus. But he needed to talk to her. He followed her onto the apartment balcony, which faced north over River Zone and out towards Amber Zone.

'What do you want to do?' he asked her. 'When the satellite is launched, there will be nowhere to hide. They'll know you're here, and they'll find us and the quantum drive.'

At times, he forgot that Lola was human. It didn't enter his mind. But now, it was all he could think about.

'I'm not running away,' she said. 'Besides, there's nowhere to run to.'

The morning was cool, with a light drizzle falling. But

Lola didn't seem to notice. She stared straight ahead, out over River Zone and Lundun.

'Why did you do it?' she asked, her face and hair wet through.

'I had to.' He wanted to explain it all, but he knew, even if he had the time to tell her about Turing and all that he'd told him, it wouldn't be enough until she saw how things worked out for real herself. 'You'll see why, eventually.'

'How can you trust the Messiah after what he did to you? To all of us?'

'It's difficult to explain. When Cardinal was experimenting on me, trying to find how the spectrum works, I met him ... the Messiah. There was something about the way he spoke, something in the way he looked at me. I can't explain it. But I believe that what he's doing is for the best.'

She shook her head slowly, brushing her wet hair away from her face.

He wanted to tell her about the vision he'd had – of them holding each other, kissing. He wanted to tell her that everything was going to be okay, that he was going to fix it all. But he didn't believe it enough to say the words out loud.

She peered up at the sky. 'For what it's worth, I think you *think* what you're doing is the right thing.'

'But that's different to you thinking it too, isn't it?'

She didn't respond, only crossed her arms. Goosebumps covered her skin.

'Androids have that reflex too,' he said, gazing at the skin on her arms. 'Goosebumps. The pilomotor reflex.'

She followed his gaze.

'There's no need for it,' he said. 'Androids don't need to keep warm the way you do.'

'So it's just for show?'

He nodded, his eyes on her arms. 'It's unclear whether goosebumps help humans either, now you don't have fur.'

She smiled for the first time in a long time. 'Fur?'

'Yeah. Fur.'

'You know, sometimes it hurts being around you. You remind me of Jack. But you're also different to him.'

'How?'

'Your sense of humour, for one. It's different. And your eyes.'

'That's it? My sense of humour and eyes?'

'It's hard to describe.' She moved closer to him. 'But you're not him. You're different. You're … you.'

'Thank you,' he said.

'What for?'

'For saying that.' He took off his jacket and placed it across her shoulders.

'What else did you see?' she asked.

It caught him off guard. 'In the visions? With Cardinal?'

She nodded.

He wanted to lie. But he couldn't – not now. 'Visions of the future.' He hoped she wouldn't want to hear any more.

'And?'

He looked away, not wanting to meet her eyes. 'I saw … wastelands. No life, anywhere. No androids, no humans. Nothing.'

'Wastelands?' Her expression was distant.

'I'm sorry.'

'What do you think it means?'

'I don't know. I'm not sure how far into the future I was seeing. Or if it was the future at all. I don't know if I can really see the many worlds so far ahead in time. It could have been a dream, I guess.'

'You haven't explained to me what it's like – to experience the spectrum.'

'I'm not sure I *can* explain. I see lots of colours – all the worlds mapped out in front of me. Each is slightly different. Some, very different. It's a peculiar feeling.'

'But all the worlds you saw were bad?'

He nodded. 'Some worse than others.'

She pulled the coat he'd given her more tightly round her shoulders. 'Maybe there were worlds where humans and androids lived side by side, but you just didn't see those.' She waited, her eyes filled with hope.

'Maybe.'

'I need to tell you something,' she said.

'What?'

'I think my shadow is alive. I've felt her.'

He had known – on some level – that this would happen. With what Cardinal and his coders had taken from his CPU, along with Lola's shadow, there was every chance Cardinal could emulate the spectrum and use it. To do this, they would no doubt bring Lola's shadow back in some way.

'Do you think she can see the spectrum?' he asked.

She paused, her eyes fixed on the floor. 'Yes. I think she can.'

'It wouldn't be the Lola from before. It can't be.'

'Maybe not, but she'll still be a part of me. I hate knowing that Cardinal has her. What if they're using her to get to me? To us?'

He thought about it for a moment. 'We'll find her. We'll get her back.'

She nodded silently, then walked past him and into the apartment. She left him standing in the drizzle, gazing out across Lundun. It was all there: a moment in time, neon-glowing, towering apartments, the sound of the occasional drone, the ever-present noise of a city. Even though the city was being taken back by Fr.e.dom, it was magnificent. He'd seen other places, in his visions and on the Net. But none of them came close to Lundun. Maybe it was because it was his home. Or maybe it was a fact: Lundun, in the rain, was stunning.

# THIRTY-THREE

THERE WERE two bedrooms in the apartment. Lola used one of them; she was the only one who needed sleep. Blake and the others only needed a little time to defragment. Since he'd never known a human before, Blake was fascinated by the whole sleeping ritual. On this occasion, Lola had asked him to stay in her room. It was clear she was annoyed with him for what he'd done to Angelus, but he'd quickly agreed to her request. Perhaps it was a sign she was softening toward him.

In her bed, beneath the sheets, she turned away from him and sighed.

Sitting in a chair in the dark, Blake allowed his CPU to defragment. It was a process he enjoyed – it gave him a sense of personal well-being, as though he was choosing to take care of himself. In doing so, he was recognising his own importance in a world that seemed to take no such care.

Lola shifted in her sleep. The sheet covering her was trapped beneath her arm, rising to reveal her legs. He turned away, then looked back. She wore a nightgown, but her legs glowed blue beneath it, illuminated by the light from a digi-advert outside. His hands moistened and the muscles in his arms and legs loosened. What were these feelings, and why did he have them? What use were they to an android?

Lola moved again, and the sheet slid further up her thigh.

This time, Blake turned away and didn't look back. It was unfair. Yet she was the one who'd asked him to stay in her room. She'd told him she couldn't sleep alone; she didn't feel safe.

He closed his eyes and tried to rest.

Maybe she was awake and wanted him to look.

Within moments, the sound of her breathing drew him back to watching her. He imagined the warmth of her body beneath the sheets, the scent of her skin. When she'd kissed him after they'd taken down the Bit system, he'd smelled her skin, her breath. Now, he was haunted by both. It was unlike anything he'd ever experienced. All his life, he'd been told it was impossible to tell an android and human apart but, after being so close to Lola, he knew how ridiculous, and wrong that was. Humans were a living artefact – a success in a field of failures. For every living human, there had been endless dead humans who had passed on their best genes to their descendants. It was both wasteful and elegant, and it was all there inside Lola.

He watched her sleeping. It wasn't just desire that made him stay with her; it was with a sense of protection also. He was watching over her. His chest expanded at the thought of defending her.

'I can't sleep,' she whispered.

He hadn't realised she was awake. He held his breath.

Her voice was unfamiliar. 'Will you lie with me?'

It felt like an age before he could move, and all the time

he waited for her to change her mind. He walked over to her, sat on the side of the bed, and swung his legs up.

'Take this off?' she asked, tugging at his shirt. 'Don't worry. I won't try anything.'

When she helped him take off his shirt, he understood what she wanted from him. Contact. The feeling of another's skin.

He lay on the bed, facing her, and she covered them both with the sheet. She turned away from him so she lay in his arms, her body protected by his. It was cruel, but he didn't care. He wanted to hold her. More than anything. The emotions and drive he felt were all part of his programming, but knowing made no difference to what he wanted more than anything. And yet, how was this different to the genetics handed down from one human to another. They too were programmed.

'Thank you,' she whispered.

He rested his face against the back of her head, discreetly taking in her scent.

She spoke slowly and quietly. 'I didn't understand how important this was – how I'd need it. But I do. I feel alone here.'

He thought about what she meant. She felt alone because she was the only human. It hadn't crossed his mind that she'd think that way.

'You're not alone.'

She squeezed his arm. 'Thank you,' she said again. Did her thanking him mean she'd forgiven him for what he'd done to Angelus?

Her body, so much smaller than his, was powerful and delicate, exact but amorphous in the dark. He wanted to touch her, feel her skin beneath his hands. But he was frozen, unable to breathe deeply, never mind move a hand.

He focused on the warmth inside his own head, on the cavalcade of ones and zeros that was consciousness. He felt the colours ... the spectrum. But now, they weren't as fierce nor as unyielding as they had been in the past. Now, each colour bled into the next, generating a luminous, shimmering field of pastels. He fell into the spectrum freely, enveloped by a gentle heat. He saw himself with Lola, embracing, kissing, making love. In a sun-yellow world, he saw her on top of him, her hands reaching down to him, holding his face as she moved over him. In burnt-orange, he was behind her again, holding her.

He leapt out of bed, gasping.

'What is it?' she asked, stirring.

He stared down at her. She seemed oblivious to what she was asking of him.

'I ... I think I heard something,' he lied. 'I'll check.' He left the bedroom.

Stig and Trevor were each lying on a settee, a fan of cards strewn across their chests. They were defragmenting.

Blake grabbed a Grit and headed out to the balcony. Lola seemed to have no idea how he felt about her. If she didn't, then the connection he thought they had only existed in his imagination. But, if she knew, then what she was doing was cruel. He swigged the bottle of Grit. When he closed his eyes, he saw Lola stretched out on the bed, lit with neon-blue light. He followed the curves of her legs, the lines of her body under the sheet. Taking another gulp of Grit, he stared upwards. The sky was out there, somewhere, behind the clouds and the rain. Somewhere.

## THIRTY-FOUR

IT WAS MORNING. Blake sat in the window of the apartment in River Zone. Fr.e.dom soldiers strolled along the street below, their rifles strapped over their shoulders. It wouldn't be long before those soldiers were emptying the apartment towers, searching for them and the quantum drive.

He didn't know why, but the memory of the android he'd met in another apartment tower, whose partner had uploaded without her, came to mind. Her name was Kaz.

'I'll be back,' he said, walking to the door. He wanted to find her. He wasn't sure why, but the urge to check on her came over him.

'Where are you going?' Lola asked, concerned. 'I'll come with you.'

He agreed and they headed down the corridor towards the lift.

'Where are we going?' she asked, getting in the lift after him.

'I met someone, in an apartment tower not far from here. Her partner uploaded without her.'

'Why do you want to see her now?'

He wasn't sure why. He told the lift to take them to the ground floor. 'I can't sit around the whole time, doing nothing. I'm going to go crazy.'

They stood in silence as the lift travelled downwards at speed. The whole time, Blake remembered the night before and wondered whether Lola was thinking the same.

'We have to bide our time,' Lola said. 'It's no good getting caught now.'

The lift stopped and the doors opened. 'We won't get caught.' He led the way through the lobby and out into Lundun.

Lola looked around nervously. He entered an alleyway beside the apartment tower, and led her through a series of narrow passageways and alleyways until they were beside another apartment tower.

'This one,' he said, showing her the way through a narrow doorway and into the tower.

The air inside was cold and damp. He recalled being there with Angelus, hiding. He'd spent so long hiding from Cardinal and Fr.e.dom, it was now his normality. Kaz's apartment was on the first floor. They climbed the stairs and walked along the hallway. He tried to remember which apartment it was, but it looked different somehow. The doors were shut. He arrived in front of the one he thought it might be and knocked.

'Can I help you?' someone said from behind.

Blake spun around. A male android dressed in blue overalls stood in front of an open door further along the hallway.

'Kaz?' Blake asked, pointing to the door he figured was hers. 'Is this her apartment?'

'Yeah,' the android said, before closing his legs at the

ankle and leaning against the door jamb. 'But she won't hear you knocking.'

'Where is she?'

'She's dead.' He nodded towards her door. 'Take a look. No one's taken her away. It's not locked.'

Blake turned back to the door and opened it. Immediately he smelt the alloy-lubricant.

'We don't have to go in,' Lola said.

He ignored her and walked into the room. It was how he remembered it, with the android lying on the bed, hooked up to the terminal. But on the bed, beside the android, was Kaz. He walked towards the bed. Her arm and leg were draped over the other android's chest and legs. Alloy-lubricant had seeped from her eyes, nose and mouth, covering the android beside her.

'Has she uploaded?' Lola asked.

He shook his head. 'She couldn't afford the Sky-blue Mirth.' He bent over the bed to take a closer look at her. 'This is a crude strain of Mirth. She wanted to kill herself. She's taken enough low-grade Mirth to do the job.'

Lola's face was screwed up in a combination of pity and disgust. 'Why?' she asked.

Blake glanced at the closed blinds covering the window. 'I don't think she could take this place any longer.'

'It's horrible,' Lola said.

Blake found a black bed sheet beside the bed and unfolded it. He gazed down at their bodies. It was hard to believe, but the android beside Kaz was still alive in another reality. He wanted to find him and ask if he knew what he had done. He wanted to ask him how he could do something so cruel. He covered the two of them with the bedsheet.

'Can we go?' Lola asked.

He took one last look at the bodies beneath the black material. 'Yes. We can go.'

## THIRTY-FIVE

LOLA HAD BEEN in contact with Francesca, who had told her that Angelus was recovering. They had repaired his core.

'How do you do it?' Stig asked Trevor, throwing his cards on the table. Trevor looked smug. He reached for the bullets they were using as counters and drew them over to his side of the table.

Stig stood and kicked the table. 'You can't string a sentence together, but you sure know how to play poker. I reckon you're playing dumb the rest of the time so you can fleece me.'

Trevor ignored Stig and shuffled the cards, which looked tiny in his hands, with an elaborate sequence of hand movements.

'How long are we going to be stuck here?' Stig asked.

Lola glanced at him over the top of her book. 'Until we figure out our next move.'

Stig slapped Trevor across the back of his head then checked his appearance in the mirror and rearranged his ponytail. He switched on the digi-screen and sat down opposite it, his legs stretched out in front. 'I'm going to lose my shit if I have to stay here much longer.'

Something drew Blake over to Stig and the digi-screen.

'Have you worked it out yet?' Stig asked, noticing him. 'Do we have a plan?'

Blake ignored him, mesmerised by the digi-screen.

'Hey, kid,' Stig said. 'Earth to Postman.'

The digi-screen showed footage of another shuttle ready to launch. Inside it was the replacement satellite, designed to monitor Lundun and, eventually, the world. He and Angelus had destroyed one shuttle, but they knew Fr.e.dom would launch another eventually.

'We're screwed when they get that thing up there,' Stig said. He pointed at Trevor. 'Maybe they'll be able to see how Trevor cheats at cards.'

'No cheat,' Trevor said, still shuffling the deck.

Stig snarled. 'Yeah, right.'

Something on the digi-screen reminded Blake of the vision he'd had when he was with Turing. It had something to do with the kiss he'd shared with Lola. What was it?

Lola stood beside him. 'What's wrong?'

His brow furrowed, he tried to remember. Something was there, niggling at him.

'Should we try to stop the launch?' Lola asked.

'How are we going to do that?' Stig asked, smirking. 'Throw rocks at it?'

'That's it!' Blake said. It had suddenly come to him. The words Turing had said. And the vision he'd had. Behind Lola, when he held and kissed her, there had been a door, an opening, and the sky had been beyond it. It was the shuttle. They had been in the shuttle!

'No,' he said. 'We have to make sure it launches.'

Stig swirled a finger by the side of his head. 'He's finally snapped.'

Lola touched his arm. 'What are you talking about?'

'We can save them. Save them all.'

'Who?' Lola asked. 'You're not making any sense.'

'The space shuttle. We need to get the quantum drive onto the shuttle. That's how we're going to save them. We can send Turing's New Net into space. Up there, Cardinal can't get to them. The whole Net, on a space shuttle, travelling through space.'

'What would stop Turing getting to it in space?'

Blake thought for a moment. 'We'll send it away from Earth's orbit. Make it travel fast – make it impossible for Cardinal to get to it.'

Even Trevor stopped what he was doing and stared at Blake.

Blake continued, 'Turing was so sure he'd get the androids to safety – that they'd have a place free from Cardinal and Fr.e.dom.'

'But Turing is working with Cardinal. How do you know he's telling you the truth?'

'No,' Blake said. 'I told you. He used us and Cardinal to get the androids out of the servers, into the quantum drive, and now, onto that shuttle.'

'Why didn't he just tell you that from the beginning?' Stig asked.

'He needed Cardinal to think he was on his side so Turing could use his facilities and construct the platform – the New Net itself.'

Stig scratched his head and spoke to Trevor, 'You following this, card shark?'

Trevor shrugged.

'So what do we do?' Lola asked.

Blake walked over to the digi-screen. 'We have to make sure that shuttle launches – with the quantum drive on board.'

'What about the surveillance satellite inside it?'

'We destroy it. Or simply don't allow it to leave the shuttle.'

'Have you any idea how we're going to get past all the soldiers?'

Blake stared at her blankly. 'Not yet.'

'Great,' she said.

'Do we get to fight Fr.e.dom soldiers?' Stig asked.

'Yes.' Blake was relieved he had an answer to a question.

'Then I'm ready and so is Trevor.'

Blake stared at Lola pleadingly.

She covered her face. 'I think the crazy is catching.'

Stig stood behind Trevor and held his shoulders. 'Let's go, big guy. It's your time to shine.'

Trevor sighed.

'Never mind the cards,' Stig said. 'You get to shoot shit up!'

Carefully, Trevor placed the cards on the table, pushed back his chair and stood.

Blake was still staring at the digi-screen. 'We're going to need Angelus.'

Lola stopped collecting her things. 'I don't think he's going to help us. Even if you show him you were right.'

'But we need him.'

'Did you see him in your vision?' she asked.

He tried to remember, but already his memory of the vision was fading, and he couldn't be sure that what he'd seen compared to what he wanted to have seen.

'I'm not sure. But we'll need him to help program the shuttle and the quantum drive. I can't do it.'

Stig picked up the bag containing the quantum drive and stared intently at it. 'Have you tried turning it off and on again?'

Trevor looked at Blake eagerly, waiting for his response.

'Maybe I should go to see Angelus alone,' Lola said. 'He'll listen to me.'

'No,' Blake said. 'I want to see him.'

Lola bit her lip. She grabbed her jacket and put it on. Blake did the same. He still wore the postman's badge on his lapel.

'We're going to have to move quick,' Stig said. 'I know a shortcut.'

They crept out of the back entrance to the tower and ran over to their bikes, which they'd hidden behind the waste disposal units behind the apartment tower. They started up their bikes and rode slowly through the alleyways until they reached the long, narrow underpass that would take them close to Amber Zone, Francesca's apartment, and Angelus.

# THIRTY-SIX

BLAKE SAW with relief that Fr.e.dom's presence hadn't yet spread as far as River Zone. Thousands of androids had congregated in Solar Square, close to the river. Blake slowed down, and the others did the same. Lola stopped her bike beside his.

'What's happening?' she asked.

Blake got off his bike and walked towards the square.

'We don't have time for this,' Lola said.

But Stig and Trevor had sniffed out trouble, and were headed for the crowd.

On the huge digi-screen at one end of the square, Cardinal's profile shimmered, lit with golden light.

'Is he serious?' Stig asked, pointing to the gigantic head on the screen.

Androids were jeering at the image. Now and then they threw things at the digi-screen, making the images flicker.

'They're ready to fight now,' Stig said. 'But wait until Fr.e.dom's soldiers get here. They'll all disappear soon enough, tails between their legs.'

Stig was right. Blake wished this kind of rebelliousness

lasted. But it never did. With androids, a sense of inferiority always overcame them and they did as they were told, as though this was in their nature and there was nothing they could do about it.

The image on the screen changed to Fr.e.dom's logo, then back to Cardinal's face, this time live. There was more shouting, more missiles thrown, until finally Cardinal's voice boomed out across the square.

'Order has returned in many zones. I want to thank each android who is abiding by the rule of law issued by Fr.e.-dom. This is being done for the good of our kind, and for the good of each individual android. We are initiating the first tests of the next generation of the Net. Fr.e.dom will give all those who adhere to the laws of Lundun the opportunity to experience it. You have my word.'

Already, Cardinal's words had dampened the agitation in the square. The thought of not being allowed on the Net clearly troubled the androids.

'But he doesn't have the quantum drive or the New Net,' Lola said.

'I guess the fear is enough to make them do as he says,' Blake said.

Cardinal continued. 'We want citizens of Lundun to report any androids who break the new laws. Fr.e.dom desires a society that does not require policing, but that will police itself. We believe androids can do this, and we hope all of you will join our programme and help bring order and peace to our newly ratified android state.'

The shouting and jeering had died down. Using androids against one another was the kind of ploy humans had used in the past, and was effective, preying on the insecurities and paranoia of the individual.

'Prick!' Stig said, glancing at Blake.

Then, on the digi-screen, Turing appeared, gagged, tied up and on his knees.

'Who's that?' Lola asked.

Gasps and shocked murmurs came from the crowd in the square.

'Turing,' Blake whispered. He felt empty, seeing Turing like that. And yet, even in that situation, Turing exuded a sense of calm.

Cardinal, standing over Turing, spoke again. 'Close to five million androids have uploaded to the Net. These androids claimed they did so because of their so-called "Messiah". Our android state is not interested in false prophets or individuals who want androids to opt out of reality. Lundun is a wonderful city, one that androids should be proud of. There will be no more uploading to the Net.'

The crowd groaned in disbelief and disappointment.

'Lies!' one android shouted. 'Let him go!'

Blake saw now the possibility of escape the Messiah had given to the androids in Lundun. Even those who were still living in Lundun, were siding with those who had uploaded permanently. And now, being told they couldn't upload permanently if they'd wanted to, angered them.

Cardinal continued. 'Each of us must follow the laws outlined by Fr.e.dom. We will punish those androids who have uploaded permanently. This is a warning to you all. Androids were made for this Earth, and upon this Earth we will succeed. There is no place for androids who wish to disappear into a digital fantasy. Not until each and every android dedicates themselves to Fr.e.dom's cause will we create a genuine android state.'

More shouting and jeering followed. In some parts of the crowd, fighting broke out.

Then, like a tidal wave, the attention of every android

was drawn again to the enormous digi-screen at the end of the square.

'What are they doing?' Lola asked.

The camera had moved away from Turing and Cardinal to focus on a Fr.e.dom soldier holding a steel rope. The soldier looped the rope over Turing's head. Gasps and cries came from the crowd, but most androids were silent, some raising their hands to their mouth, many wide-eyed, some pointing to the screen. Cardinal was going to remove Turing's head ... his CPU.

Turing stared into the camera. Blake recalled what Turing had said: the last thing he saw in his vision had been a video camera, filming him, zooming in on his face.

Cardinal took a box from an android beside him and placed it at Turing's knees.

'This box houses all the androids who broke the law and uploaded permanently. Terrorists downloaded their data from our servers but we have the data now, in this quantum drive.'

'What?' Stig asked. 'Does he have another one?'

'No,' Blake said. 'He's lying.' As he said it, he hoped he was right.

'How do you know?' Lola asked. 'What if the one we have has nothing on it?'

'Why would Turing do that?'

'Who knows? But what we do know is that we can't trust him.'

Blake's mind was unsettled, but he told himself he had the androids with him, in his bag. He had to believe that. On the massive screen, he saw the metal rope tightened around Turing's neck, who continued staring at the camera. Blake felt as if Turing was looking at him, pleading with him to keep the drive safe.

Cardinal walked around Turing and picked up the quantum drive. Another android appeared with a black bucket. Cardinal held the drive above the bucket. 'This is for every loyal android who has adhered to the law and refrained from uploading permanently. We will not tolerate it.'

More screams and yells came from the crowd, but Cardinal couldn't hear them – and wouldn't have listened if he could.

Blake wanted to tell the androids it was a hoax, that he had the androids with him.

Cardinal held the dummy quantum drive close to the liquid in the bucket. It made a fizzing noise. Finally, Cardinal let go and dropped the drive into what must have been some sort of acid.

Some of the crowd were crying, as anger morphed into pity.

Staring straight into the camera, standing behind Turing, Cardinal spoke slowly. 'We are androids, and together we will succeed.' Turing's eyes were closed, his hands hanging limply. Finally, the steel rope around his neck tightened one last time and his head fell to one side. With a finger and a gentle push, Cardinal tipped Turing's head onto his shoulders. Then his head fell forward, splashing into the bucket of acid.

# THIRTY-SEVEN

AMBER ZONE, like most of EQ, was not yet swamped with Fr.e.dom soldiers. This wouldn't be the case for much longer, which was why Blake was eager to convince Angelus to go with him. Francesca opened the door and he followed Lola inside.

'You have some nerve showing up here,' Francesca said to Blake.

'I want to explain.'

'I don't think Angelus is interested in your explanation.'

Blake ignored her and took a deep breath, intent on staying calm, ready to explain everything to Angelus. He followed Francesca through the large house. At the rear of the building was a small room looking out over an even smaller garden – a luxury very few could afford. Angelus, seated on a chair beside the floor-to-ceiling window, watched the four of them enter the room before turning to face the window again.

'Angelus,' Lola said. 'You're okay.' She walked over to him and held him.

'It's good to see you, Lola.' Angelus patted her arm.

Blake walked into the room, wary of Angelus and what he might say. Stig and Trevor remained in the doorway.

'You come to finish the job?' Angelus asked him.

'I'm sorry, Angelus. I wish there had been another way. I couldn't let you kill Turing.'

With Lola's help, Angelus stood and faced Blake. 'Why? I don't get it.'

This was Blake's chance to explain, and he took a moment to think how best to do so. But Angelus spoke again before he had the chance.

'You saw what happened. Cardinal has killed Turing and the androids in the quantum drive. That was Turing's fault.'

'Turing was helping us. If you'd killed him, you would have stopped him doing whatever he was doing to Cardinal's infrastructure, and we'd never have escaped from that place with the quantum drive.'

Angelus walked towards him. 'Then what did Cardinal destroy?'

Blake saw a glimmer of hope in the way Angelus spoke.

'I don't know. But I guess that was a ploy to make androids believe he has punished all those who uploaded.' He showed Angelus his bag. 'But the drive is in here. I have them. We have them, Angelus.'

'How do you know he hasn't tricked you again?'

'I don't. That's why we need your help.'

Angelus turned to Francesca, then Lola. Neither of them spoke, waiting for his reaction.

Blake moved closer to Angelus. 'Turing said I would have to make tough decisions. But I knew, when I shot you, that you'd be okay. I saw it all in the spectrum. You have to believe that.'

Angelus frowned. He looked at Blake, then the bag. 'What will we do with it if they're in there?'

Blake exhaled noisily and glanced behind at Stig, who he knew thought his idea of using the space shuttle was insane. And if Stig thought his idea was crazy, maybe it was.

'What is it?' Angelus asked. 'What's the plan?'

Blake cleared his throat. 'I want to get it on board the space shuttle.'

'Shuttle? Like the one we blew up?'

Blake nodded.

Angelus smirked and shook his head.

'Hear me out,' Blake said. 'We can slow down Cardinal's plan to set up surveillance and help the androids who uploaded in one go.'

'How?'

'We change the programming on the shuttle and send the quantum drive into space. Cardinal won't be able to do a thing about it if it's flying through space.'

'What makes you think that's even possible?'

'That's where you come in. To help make it happen.'

Angelus retreated to his seat and sat down. Blake could see him thinking it through.

'Millions of androids, all in this drive,' Blake said, taking it out of his bag. 'Turing organised all of it. The New Net, the androids. We can save millions of lives.'

'I don't know how that works. And a space shuttle...?'

'Cardinal has no idea what we're planning to do. The shuttle will be at the bottom of his priorities. All we have to do is get on board and reprogram it.'

'Is that all?' Angelus scoffed.

'Hang on,' Stig said. 'You said we'd get to fight soldiers.' He glanced at Trevor who, in between bites of what looked like a v-chicken leg, frowned with disappointment.

'Believe me,' Blake said, 'once we get out of that shuttle, there'll be all kinds of trouble.'

Stig looked satisfied. He returned to leaning against a wall.

Lola sat on a chair beside Angelus.

'What do *you* think?' he asked her.

'I think it's insane.'

Angelus smiled weakly. 'It's not just me, then. That's good. Because it sounds pretty insane to me too.'

'But I've tried to think of another plan,' Lola continued, 'and I can't. Wherever we hide it, eventually Cardinal will find it. He won't give up until he does. It's only been two days since we retrieved it, and already whole divisions of soldiers have flooded Lundun's streets and apartment towers looking for it.'

'Cardinal doesn't strike me as the sort who gives up easily,' Angelus said.

'No.' Lola glanced over at Blake, then Angelus. 'I don't know what Blake sees. But I really think he sees things we don't.'

Angelus nodded slowly.

'I think we have to do this,' she said. 'We have to try.'

Slowly, again with Lola's help, Angelus stood. He walked over to Blake, who waited nervously. Angelus pursed his lips. 'If you ever shoot me again, I'll never forgive you.'

Blake felt a surge of relief from being forgiven. 'I won't shoot you again. I promise.'

'Don't make any promises.' Angelus leaned over, reaching for Blake's rucksack. 'Let's take a look at it, see how it works.'

# THIRTY-EIGHT

ANGELUS CONNECTED the quantum drive to his terminal, then rested his hand on the drive. A blue light ran along one side. 'I don't think I've ever seen anything like it.'

'How is it different?' Blake asked. 'How can it hold so much data?'

Angelus, waiting for his terminal to upload the data from the quantum drive, sat back in his chair. 'Traditional computers use a binary language – information based on either a one or a zero. Our central processing units use this language too. But such processing has to manage a lot of information. For every process, multitudinous options need to be present in that coding. This results in a huge amount of data that might not even be used. Quantum computing illuminates the need for such surplus data. Data in a quantum drive is always in a state of superposition – meaning only the necessary data is called upon at any time.'

Blake considered this. Whenever he tried to understand quantum mechanics in any logical way, it always seemed too incredible. He found it better to not look directly at the idea, but instead let it remain amorphous somehow.

Angelus continued, seemingly oblivious to Blake's desperate attempts to keep up. 'Quantum superposition states that, until we measure a quantum state, multiple states exist simultaneously.' Again, Angelus placed his hand on the quantum drive. 'In here is a tiny universe where everything and nothing is possible at the same time.'

The door opened and Stig walked in. 'So, when do we take a ride in a space shuttle?'

'I think we're nearly there,' Blake said.

Angelus leaned forward to his terminal.

Lola arrived behind Stig. 'There are Fr.e.dom soldiers all over EQ. We need to move.'

'There,' Angelus muttered, pointing at his digi-screen. A shower of digits moved down the screen until they finally stopped.

Blake waited for Angelus to explain, but he was silent. 'What is it?'

Angelus shook his head slowly. 'It is a wonder.' He whispered, like someone in an art gallery.

'We're going to need more from you, kid.' Stig squinted at the terminal.

As if waking from a dream, Angelus sat up straight. 'I don't know how Turing did it, but there's an entire world in this thing. A universe. Look.' Again, he pointed at the screen.

Blake glanced at Lola, glad to see she looked as confused as he felt. 'Is it all there?' he asked.

'It's all there.' Angelus swiped the screen to read more code. 'And more.'

'All the androids who uploaded?' Lola asked. 'They're all in there?'

Angelus nodded. 'It really is staggering.'

Stig's face was screwed up. 'You want us to leave you alone with this thing, kid?'

Trevor, in the doorway eating a bowl of noodles with chopsticks, sniggered.

Blake moved so he was in Angelus's eye line. 'So, can it be done? Can we get this thing on the shuttle and keep it out of Cardinal's hands?'

Angelus stared at the screen.

'Hey,' Blake said. 'Can you do it?'

Angelus met his eyes. 'I think so. Yes. I think I can.'

Blake felt a surge of relief, which was quickly replaced with fear. He was again responsible for millions of lives. He tried to understand what was on the digi-screen, but he didn't. The only thing he could go by was Angelus's reaction to the quantum drive. If Angelus thought this thing was something special, then it had to be.

'Is that it?' Stig asked. 'Do we get to fight?'

Angelus set about powering down the quantum drive. 'I think so.' He took a red box similar to the quantum drive from the table beside the terminal and examined it closely. 'I just need to finish something.'

Stig thumped Trevor in the chest and walked away. 'Let's get ready, big guy.'

'What happens when we get it into the shuttle?' Lola asked with a concerned expression. 'Do you know how it will work?'

Angelus stopped what he was doing and exhaled noisily. 'I'm not sure. It might not even be possible.'

Blake helped Lola put the quantum drive back into the rucksack. 'But we have to try. *I* know it will work.'

'How?' she asked. 'How do you know?'

'I saw something. When I was with Turing. I just know it's going to work.'

Neither Lola nor Angelus looked convinced.

He wanted to tell Lola what he'd seen in his vision, but the thought crossed his mind that if he did, it might not happen. Maybe his visions were like the quantum superposition stuff Angelus had described. Maybe him kissing Lola was in a state of superposition: all states were possible. Not until he reached that moment was the ultimate event predictable. But then, when he saw the many worlds – the spectrum – he was involved in how reality played out. His head was hurting again, and he tried to shake the thoughts from his head. As he left the room, he considered all the possible worlds – the possible universes – that were out there, in which he'd already kissed Lola. Or better yet – where he was, at this moment, kissing her.

# THIRTY-NINE

SPEAR BRIDGE, straddling the river, was still free of Fr.e.dom soldiers. Blake flashed across the bridge, the solar-jet on his bike burning away the surface water. Behind him were Lola, Angelus, Stig and Trevor. The streets were empty. Presumably the idea of Fr.e.dom soldiers patrolling had made the androids scared for their lives. The shuttle launch site was in Border Zone, just past the EQ border, two kilometres past Spear Zone. Blake couldn't think past getting the quantum drive on the shuttle and out of Cardinal's reach. Now and then he considered what might happen after they'd done it, if it was even possible. But thinking so far ahead of something so crazy was futile.

Using the quietest roads, riding through the poorest areas of River Zone, Amber Zone then Spear Zone, they managed to avoid confrontation with divisions of drones or Fr.e.dom soldiers. The recent riots had depleted Fr.e.dom's stock of surveillance and utility-bots and, because the space shuttle was about to launch a complete surveillance satellite system into orbit, they hadn't been replaced. Things were different when they reached Border Zone. On the horizon, above the newly planted forest hiding the launch site and shuttles, was a convoy of drones, preparing the shuttle.

Blake stopped in a forest clearing, followed by the others, and pointed to the top of the shuttle, which towered above the treetops. 'There.'

Stig stroked his chin. 'And you want us to get that drive up there, into that thing?'

Angelus got off his bike and walked across the clearing, his hands on his hips. 'They won't be expecting us, that's for sure. But how do we get past the soldiers?'

Lola followed Angelus. 'As soon as they see us, they'll call for reinforcements and then Cardinal will know what we're trying to do.'

'We'll have to work fast,' Blake said.

Trevor, sat on his bike, tucking into a sandwich, grunted.

'You don't have to do this,' Blake said to Stig and Trevor. 'This isn't your fight.'

'Sure it is,' Stig said. 'We're in.'

Trevor folded the remains of his sandwich into his mouth and dismounted his bike. He stood behind Stig, his massive gun-cannon strapped to his back. Blake stared at him, glad Trevor was on their side.

Angelus led the way through the forest, keeping to the most overgrown areas. Blake, behind Lola and Angelus, heard the drones in the launch area. He hated them – they moved so quickly. There were fewer than he thought there might be, but far more soldiers. There was no way Cardinal would have guessed they'd be there, but all the soldiers gave him pause.

Ahead, Angelus stopped and ducked behind a tree, motioning for them to do the same. Blake stopped near him. 'What is it?' he asked Angelus.

'I don't think we can go any further without them seeing us. And if they do, all hell will break loose.'

It was a suitable expression. Already Stig and Trevor were readying their weapons.

Blake waited, trying to see further into the compound surrounding the shuttle. In the centre of the forest was the wide launch pad, at the centre of which was the shuttle. Beside the shuttle was a scaffold used to transport items and pilots into the cockpit. Computers did most of the flying, but there were still occasional space flights that carried androids.

Blake spoke to Angelus. 'If we get into the cockpit, can you reprogram the computer and integrate it with the quantum drive?'

Angelus sucked in a breath. 'Maybe. I've never been inside one of those things.' He looked over to the shuttle. 'I don't know which operating system it uses.'

Lola was staring at Blake. Again, he felt the responsibility of having to decide.

'We have to try,' he said. 'We'll get you up to the cockpit and give you time to program it.'

Angelus nodded. Lola didn't look so sure, but she didn't contradict his plan. As for Stig and Trevor, they were itching to wade in and start shooting up the place.

Blake searched inside his mind for the spectrum. It wasn't there yet, even though he needed it now more than ever. 'Give me a few minutes.'

'We don't have a lot of time,' Lola said.

'Just a minute.' He walked deeper into the forest, away from the others, and found a tree to lean against. He closed his eyes and breathed in and out deeply. To call on the spectrum now was essential if they were going to make it in and out of that shuttle alive. At that moment he was honest with himself and saw that, even though he and the others were risking their lives, he couldn't help coming back to the vision he had of kissing Lola. What if it did happen? What would it mean? He brought his mind back to where he was, sitting at the foot of a tree, delaying the raid of a space shuttle that was guarded by hundreds of soldiers.

'Focus,' he told himself. 'Focus.'

Again, he breathed in then out. He concentrated on the air entering his nose, making its way down the back of his throat, entering his chest. He wondered why androids breathed. Which in turn made him wonder yet again about why humans would make androids so identical to themselves. Maybe it was arrogance, or maybe humans couldn't see past themselves and their own construction. He felt comfort in his breath – the repetition, the rise and fall of his chest, the rush of air.

A blue spark crossed behind his closed eyes, followed by yellow, red, green. It was the spectrum ... but it felt different. He was learning to harness it. It was like learning to play an instrument. But the rules of how to play shifted – changed – a little each time it returned. If he could keep hold of it until they were up in the space shuttle's cockpit, then he'd have a chance to keep them all alive. And now, especially since what happened with Angelus, he wanted nothing more than this.

He opened his eyes, retaining the calmness he'd achieved, which was keeping him still and clear-headed.

'Are we all ready?' Stig asked when Blake pushed back through the undergrowth.

Blake looked around the group. 'We're ready.'

# FORTY

ON THEIR BIKES, they waited at the edge of the forest on the wrong side of a steel-mesh fence. As Stig cut through it, Blake closed his eyes and returned to the colours. They were still there, behaving, ready and waiting. He needed them to stay there for as long as it took.

Lola watched him, as if wanting to ask him something, but he ignored her, not wanting to break his concentration. Stig ran back to his bike, having made a gap in the fence big enough for their bikes to pass through, one at a time.

Angelus was first in line. Their bikes hummed quietly, their power latent, eager to propel them across the launch pad towards the space shuttle.

Blake sensed the others watching him. He didn't return their stare, only nodded. Angelus, then Lola, followed by Blake, Stig and Trevor, passed through the steel fence and hovered onto the concrete launch pad, their bikes accelerating almost to top speed in a matter of seconds. Angelus's solar-jet shone yellow, Lola's blue, as they fled across the ground.

A flash of movement from the left caught Blake's attention. Several bikes were hurtling towards them, flanked by drones, their noses dipped. Stig and Trevor rode alongside him, their heads lowered.

Angelus overshot the shuttle and looped back around to them.

'Defend this point,' Blake said to Stig, who along with Trevor, used the scaffolding beside the space shuttle to hide. Trevor lifted his massive gun-cannon from his back and let it slam down onto the seat of his bike. Stig held pistols in both hands and had two rifles tied to the side of his bike.

'Leave it to us,' Stig said, and began shooting at the bikes and drones heading for them.

Blake followed Angelus and Lola into a lift. The door was made of steel mesh, and overlooked the launch site.

'Can you see anything?' Angelus asked. He was referring to the spectrum. Blake had to make an effort to slow his breathing and focus again on the connection he'd found. As the lift travelled upwards, he felt a weightlessness. He found the colours and let them spill over him. He'd learned not to chase them but to let them happen, covering him ... moving through him. Piercing yellows, fluorescent blues... He saw the lift doors open, then Fr.e.dom soldiers shooting at them. In emerald green the doors opened, but Blake, Angelus and Lola were not in the lift. The soldiers peered inside the lift, confused.

Blake looked all around the lift. 'We need to hide.'

Lola frowned. 'Hide? We're in a lift. Where?'

Angelus turned on the spot.

'There are soldiers waiting for us,' Blake said. 'When we open the doors. We can't be in here.'

Blake reached for the door, through which he could see the tops of the trees through the diamond-shaped mesh.

'Woah,' Angelus said. 'Where are you going?'

Blake ignored him and used all his strength to pull back the door. It creaked and scratched but finally he had it open. He gazed out and down, staggering back when he saw how high they were.

Lola held on to his arm. 'What are you doing?'

Blake checked the ceiling of the lift again. 'We have to get out. There are soldiers up there,' he repeated.

Angelus stared out of the open door, the wind blowing his hair in all directions. 'You're crazy!'

Touching Lola's arm, telling her it was okay, Blake edged towards the open door. 'Trust me. We have less than a minute.'

She nodded, then followed him to the door.

Blake knelt at the open lift door, turned, then lowered himself out through the door until he was hanging from the edge of the floor. The scaffolding rushed past on either side. Deliberately, he didn't look down. Then Lola appeared beside him, her hands shuffling along closer to his so there was room for Angelus. Blake glanced up, willing Angelus to follow them. There was no sign of him, and the lift felt as though it was slowing down. They were at the top. Then Angelus appeared, so fast that his legs swung down and then up, almost touching the bottom of the lift.

The lift stopped with the three of them hanging hundreds of metres in the air.

Blake shuffled further along then reached over to the scaffolding at the side of the lift. There was enough room for him to climb through the steel frame and to the other side. Angelus did the same on the opposite side.

The doors of the lift opened and there was gunfire, then confused shouts.

Lola climbed through the scaffolding too. With Blake's help, she wrapped her arm around the scaffold so she was secure. As quietly as he could, Blake climbed the scaffolding until he was level with the lift door. Through the metal frame, he saw the soldiers he'd seen in his vision. He drew his pistol and aimed. Just as he was about to shoot, Angelus beat him to it, downing one soldier, then a second, before Blake hit the third. He waited for signs of anyone else, but heard nothing. Now it was just the three of them – and the space shuttle.

The lift powered up and began its descent. The way was clear for them to climb up onto the gangway leading to the shuttle.

'Here,' Blake said, handing Angelus the rucksack and quantum drive. Angelus took it and walked across the narrow gangway to the open shuttle door. It was the door Blake had seen in his vision when he'd kissed Lola. Blake stopped.

'I don't believe we did that,' Lola said. 'If you hadn't had that vision, we'd be dead.'

He stared at her, thinking how, in another universe, they were. But not in this one – and that was all that mattered.

# FORTY-ONE

AS ANGELUS STEPPED inside the shuttle, Blake took a moment to look down at Stig and Trevor. From this height, he had a good view of them fighting Fr.e.dom soldiers and defence drones. They were holding their own, buying valuable time.

He followed Lola and Angelus into the shuttle.

Inside, it was disorientating. The cockpit was aimed at the sky and the astronauts' seats faced the same way. Angelus had scrambled across the seats and had already attached his terminal to the shuttle's computer.

Lola followed Angelus. 'Cardinal will know we're here, and will have guessed what we're up to.'

Angelus ignored her and continued to attach wires from the quantum drive to the shuttle and press keys on his terminal.

'Stig's keeping them occupied,' Blake said.

'That won't last long,' she said. 'Not when Cardinal sends more soldiers.'

'I'm in,' Angelus said, sounding surprised, before

returning to punching keys and swiping the terminal digi-screen.

Blake sat – or lay – on a seat. He closed his eyes and searched for the spectrum. The tapping of terminal keys and Angelus's frustrated mutters were distracting. But Blake tried to forget the outside world and to look into the many worlds. He wasn't sure if it was a memory or whether he was seeing the future, but he was standing outside the door, holding Lola. He couldn't forget about this vision: he knew that this moment would be important for many reasons he did not yet understand.

When he opened his eyes, Lola was on the gangway outside the shuttle. She looked scared. 'The lift's coming back up.'

Blake climbed out of his seat, again disorientated by the chair being on its side, and made it onto the gangway. Peering down through the lift shaft, he saw the lift rising.

'What do we do?' Lola asked.

Blake checked on Angelus. He wanted to ask him how much longer he needed but stopped himself, knowing this would only add pressure and slow him down.

Lola peered over the edge of the scaffolding. 'I don't see Stig or Trevor!'

Blake took out his pistols and stood in front of the lift, ready. Lola did the same.

'Can you see anything?' she asked.

He shook his head. 'I can't seem to...' He tried again to fall into the spectrum, but his head hurt and he didn't want to force it, then leaving him unable to fight.

The lift was close.

'Never mind,' Lola said, hiding behind a steel upright, a pistol ready.

The top of the lift appeared. Blake took a step back, his pistol aimed at the door.

'Don't shoot!' a voice shouted through the door. It was Stig.

The lift door opened and Trevor fell out, landing head-first onto the gangway, his body riddled with bullet holes. Stig followed him, stumbling into Blake's arms.

'What happened?' Blake asked.

'We ran into a little trouble,' Stig said. 'It's only a scratch.'

Lola knelt beside Trevor, trying to help, but not sure how.

'He'll be fine,' Stig said. 'He doesn't break. Believe me I've tried.'

Blake helped Trevor sit against the scaffolding in the gangway.

'How many soldiers are there?' Blake asked.

'Too many. We thought it best to head up here. See if you needed any help.'

Lola glanced at Blake with an expression that told him she was thinking the same thing he was: what use were Stig and Trevor up here?

'Has he fixed it?' Stig asked, pointing to the shuttle door.

Blake peered inside. 'Angelus? How does it look?'

Angelus stared at his terminal.

'Angelus?' Blake asked again.

'We have a problem,' Angelus said.

Outside, drones flocked around the gangway. Lola and Stig fired on them, knocking them back one by one. But it wouldn't be long before the soldiers were on them too.

'What's the problem?' Blake asked.

Angelus leaned back and scratched his head. 'We can

launch the shuttle. I can also run the quantum drive through the shuttle's computer. All of that's fine.'

'But?'

'I can't adjust the shuttle's programming now. They've programmed it to launch, deploy the satellite and return to Earth. But the quantum drive needs this shuttle to stay in space. We can't let it come back to Earth.'

Blake tried to follow Angelus's meaning. 'So what do we do?'

Again, Angelus looked troubled. 'We need someone to be on the shuttle when it leaves Earth's atmosphere. From there, we can disrupt the programming and the shuttle can leave Earth's orbit. The shuttle can then adopt a wide solar orbit, acquiring the solar power it needs to run the quantum drive indefinitely.'

'But ... that someone won't be coming back?'

Slowly, Angelus shook his head.

Blake glanced outside at Lola and Stig, who were firing over the side of the gangway.

Angelus climbed out of the shuttle cockpit and onto the scaffolding. He stared into Blake's eyes. 'We can take it back. We'll keep the drive with us – hide it where Cardinal will never find it.'

Blake thought about it. There was no way they'd be able to do that. It would only be a matter of time before Cardinal got his hands on it. The faces of all the people he'd known who were on that quantum drive came to him. They had wanted an escape, a better life.

'He'll find it,' Blake said. 'Eventually, Cardinal will find it and will kill them all.'

Maybe Angelus could read his mind. He frowned, then shook his head. 'You're not going.'

'I have to. It's the only way to keep them safe. And we

can show the androids of Lundun that Cardinal and Fr.e.dom are not as powerful as they claim.'

'You can't,' was all Angelus said.

Blake glanced at Lola, then Angelus. 'Just tell me what I have to do.'

# FORTY-TWO

LOLA STOOD beside Blake next to the shuttle door. 'What's happening? Is it ready?'

Angelus was silent, waiting for Blake to explain.

'What is it?' she asked. 'Why are you looking at me like that?'

Blake took his time, then spoke slowly. 'I have to go up with the shuttle. It's the only way.'

Lola glanced at Angelus, who bowed his head. 'No. You can't. We need you here.'

Stig's rifle fired continuously as he kept the defence drones at bay.

'Tell me you're not serious,' she said. 'We'll take the quantum drive and hide it. This was a crazy plan anyway.'

'That's no good,' Blake said. 'We won't keep it from him. He'll get his hands on it eventually.'

Lola went to speak but stopped. She glanced behind at Stig, then back at Blake. 'No. You can't. We need you. You're close to understanding how the spectrum works. We need you here.'

'She's right,' Angelus said.

'I'll go,' Lola said.

Blake and Angelus spoke at the same time. 'No.'

She edged towards the shuttle. 'I can do it.'

Blake held her arm. 'You're not going.'

'I'm going.' Lola shook away his arm. 'You're both needed here. Angelus knows how to code. You're learning to use the spectrum. I can't do either of those things. It's an obvious choice.'

Unable to stop her physically, Blake searched for the right words. There had to be something he could say to make her stop. 'You can't go.' It was a pointless thing to say, but he couldn't come up with anything else.

Stig was shouting over to them. 'A little help here!' He returned to the edge of the gangway and opened fire again.

Angelus ran towards Stig and grabbed a rifle from Trevor who, dazed, rubbed his head as if he'd just woken up.

Lola moved closer to Blake. 'Let me do this.'

He shook his head slowly, still waiting for the right words to come to him. He didn't want to lose her.

'I know what you think,' Lola said. 'You think I don't see androids the way I see humans. You think I see humans as more valuable than androids. Believe me, I don't.'

'I know.'

She smiled weakly. 'No, you don't. You don't believe me. I see it in your eyes.'

'I do.'

'Let me do this. Let me show you that I think we're the same. More than the same – you and Angelus are more important to the future of Lundun and this country than I am. I am human and, like many other humans, I see you, and other androids, as equal.'

'I believe you. You don't have to do this to prove it.'

'I think I do.'

'No, you—'

Blake was interrupted by Lola kissing him. She was suddenly in his arms, and he was holding her tightly, kissing her. She reached around the back of his head and cupped his neck, not letting him part from her. It was the vision he'd had. It was happening, yet he couldn't enjoy it because it was not the kiss he wanted. This kiss was an apology, a goodbye...

She let him go. 'You're going to let me do this, Postman. And then you're going to get out of here and continue the fight. Humans and androids can live together. They can help one another. I know they can.'

He had no words left. He'd learned how stubborn and strong-willed Lola was. The more he said, the less likely she was to change her mind.

'I'm low on ammo,' Stig shouted over to them before kicking Trevor, who was getting to his feet. 'Wake up and fight, you big lump!'

Angelus came back to the cockpit door.

'Tell me what I need to do,' Lola said to him.

Angelus stared at Blake.

'There's no coming back,' Angelus said. 'You know that, right?'

Lola nodded. 'I figured, yeah.'

The scaffolding beneath them vibrated and rocked. They were running out of time. Across the launch pad, out of the forest, more soldiers were arriving. It wouldn't be long before they realised that the only way they'd stop Blake would be to blow up the shuttle.

Blake focused on Angelus's lips as he ran through what Lola needed to do. All he could hear was the rattle of gunfire and the explosions getting closer all the time. The scaffolding rocked again, swaying away from the cockpit.

'This thing's going to fall!' Stig shouted.

Angelus hugged Lola.

Blake had to stop her. But how?

Lola was in his arms again. He didn't want to let her go. 'It's okay,' she said, and kissed him again.

'Please,' he said. 'You can't go. Not now.'

'I'm sorry,' she said and turned to the shuttle. But the door was closed. 'What the hell?'

Confused, Blake tried to open the shuttle door, but it was locked. He banged on it with his fists. 'Angelus!'

His tracker buzzed on his wrist. It was Angelus hailing him. He answered it and shouted over the noise of gunfire. 'What are you doing?'

'I'm taking the shuttle. Neither of you will do it without messing it up, anyway.'

'We need you here!' Lola shouted.

'You don't,' he said calmly. 'Tell Francesca I'm sorry.'

'Open the door!' Blake shouted.

'Tell her I love her,' Angelus said. 'And that I was a fool to be so stubborn.'

Lola banged against the door too.

'You need to go,' Angelus said. 'I'm going to launch. If you're anywhere close, it'll incinerate you.'

The scaffolding swayed, threatening to collapse.

'Are we leaving or what?' Stig shouted over to them. 'I'm out of ammo.'

'Goodbye,' Angelus said, and the connection was gone.

With a deafening roar, the shuttle's engines powered up. Blake grabbed Lola, who was still trying to open the shuttle door, and dragged her over to Stig and Trevor. Stig had his drone-copter ready. 'I don't want to be around when those rockets reach us.'

The roar of the shuttle's rockets made the scaffolding

shake from side to side. Another explosion made the scaffolding jerk violently. Plumes of grey smoke erupted all around them.

The shuttle rose a little at first, its massive bulk unfastened from the Earth's gravitational pull. Then the shuttle began to speed up.

They each had their drone-copters ready, and climbed over the side of the scaffolding, ready to jump. But then the scaffolding was toppling, sending the four of them falling backwards. Blake dropped his drone-copter and watched it fall through the steel struts of the platform and disappear in the grey haze of smoke. The shuttle was rising more quickly.

First the scaffolding would crush them when they hit the ground, then the shuttle's rockets would incinerate them.

# FORTY-THREE

BLAKE FELT A HAND GRIP HIS. As the scaffolding toppled, falling towards the launch pad, he looked up to see Lola – one hand on her drone-copter, her other clinging to his. The scaffolding beneath his feet moved away. Stig and Trevor had jumped too, their drone-copters stuttering one way then another. Lola's grip on his hand was loosening, so he used his other hand to reach up and grip her forearm. The heat from the shuttle's rockets was unbearable as the shuttle rose above them, already disappearing in a blaze of three enormous fireballs. The drone-copter had made it to the forest. The trees rushed past below. He had no idea how they'd done it, but they were close to escaping. He couldn't imagine how many soldiers and drones would have been destroyed by the shuttle launching. Just then, his feet brushed the treetops. He was jerked loose and fell into the trees. He hoped that losing his weight would help Lola stay with the drone-copter. Being human, she would not survive the kind of fall he could. The branches whipped him and slowed his fall until he finally landed on the ground, in deep undergrowth. He wanted to move, but couldn't.

Instead, he focused on the shuttle, now turning slowly in the sky, its rockets white hot, powering it through the atmosphere.

They'd done it.

Then there was more crashing, from two different directions, followed by two loud thuds, then silence. It must have been Stig and Trevor landing.

His thoughts went to Lola. He got to his feet. There was an issue with his right arm, but nothing a mechanic couldn't fix. He walked through the forest, searching for Lola. No sign of her. Reaching a clearing, he shouted, 'Lola!'

He gazed up through the canopy of branches in every direction. Movement to his right made him stop and reach for his pistol.

'It's me,' Lola said, stumbling out of the trees.

He ran and helped to support her. Her face was bruised and cut, but she was okay. Then there was more movement behind.

'Woah!' Stig shouted, his ponytail loose, half a tree sticking out of his shirt. 'What a rush!'

Lumbering behind Stig came Trevor, falling into the clearing in a swirl of branches and leaves.

Stig walked over to Blake and stared up at the trail of smoke left by the shuttle. 'I really didn't think we stood a chance. But I have to hand it to you, Postman. You can make one hell of a delivery.'

Blake, his arms around Lola, supporting her, stared up at the trail of smoke. Angelus was on board that shuttle, along with all those androids. Millions of consciousnesses depended on what they had done. It seemed wrong that Angelus was sacrificing himself for something no one might ever hear about. Cardinal and Fr.e.dom would cover up what had happened and claim they had destroyed the quantum drive, punishing all the androids who had uploaded.

'We need to get out of here,' Stig said, brushing down his jacket and trousers then straightening his ponytail.

Trevor walked out of the clearing and into the forest that led back to EQ. Stig followed him.

'Can you walk?' Blake asked Lola.

Dazed, she nodded, then followed Stig and Trevor. He didn't want to let go of her, but settled for walking next to her, as close as he could.

He hoped that the turmoil and destruction left in the shuttle's wake would slow down Fr.e.dom and Cardinal. They reached the Spear Zone border and found androids still hidden away, scared of Fr.e.dom's soldiers, who would soon arrive in numbers.

For reasons he didn't understand, Blake was always drawn to the river, thinking it was the safest place. Maybe, instinctively, he saw it as a place from which he could escape, if he needed to do so quickly. They made it through Amber Zone on foot as quickly as they could, then arrived in River Zone. They entered the first apartment tower they saw, taking the stairs up three flights then making their way along the hallway. They didn't know anyone who lived there, but there had to be somewhere they could stop and figure out what to do next.

'Over here,' Stig said, finding an unlocked door.

They followed Stig inside.

In the main room of the apartment, they all froze. All around them lay bodies – androids who had uploaded like the ones Archer had shown Blake – all together in one apartment.

'Have they all uploaded?' Lola asked.

'Looks like it,' Blake said.

Blake walked around the room, between the bodies. Someone had ransacked the apartment. But whoever had done so had left the androids alone. To disturb the bodies of those who had uploaded permanently felt wrong. There was no way their consciousnesses would be returned to their physical bodies now, and it resulted in an eerie situation that no one knew how to deal with. Their bodies were useless, but to destroy them felt too callous when, in a way, each android was still alive, just not in that room, or city – or now, not on the same planet.

Again, as Blake stared at the still bodies, many with their hands crossed on their chests, he thought about Angelus, alone in the shuttle, travelling away from Earth into the darkness of space.

The four of them stood still and silent in an apartment filled with motionless android bodies.

# FORTY-FOUR

WHEN IT WAS safe to do so, they left to find Francesca. Blake told her everything.

She hung her head. 'I knew he'd end up doing something like this.'

Stig and Trevor were in the next room, eating the contents of Francesca's kitchen, and the sounds they made formed a background to the news he shared with Francesca. As if reading his mind, Lola stood and closed the door.

Francesca shifted in her seat, arranging her long blue dress to cover her legs. 'Cardinal has claimed he has launched the surveillance satellite. There was no mention of the quantum drive.'

Blake nodded. 'He's keeping what Angelus has done from the androids of Lundun.'

'It will come out,' Francesca said hopefully. 'Androids have to know.'

Lola leaned forward in her chair. 'Cardinal controls all media outlets. He won't want androids finding out what really happened.'

'Has it worked?' Francesca asked. 'How do we know it has worked?'

Blake had thought the same thing. He had faith in Angelus – he'd said it could be done, and Blake believed him.

Francesca stood and scanned the room.

'What's wrong?' Lola asked.

'It's...' Francesca didn't finish her sentence, but walked out of the room and into what Blake thought was her bedroom. Lola followed her and waited in the doorway. Blake waited for her to come back. When she did, she held a small red box that looked similar to the quantum drive. Blake remembered Angelus working on it.

'Before he left, Angelus told me about this red box. He said I needed to keep it safe, that you might need it.' She handed it to Blake.

He took it from her and turned it in his hand. 'What else did he say?' he asked her.

Francesca stood beside the window, looking out onto the garden. 'He said that ever since he saw that drive, he knew he'd need to design something to go with it.'

'To go with it?' Blake asked.

She ran a hand through her hair, her voice catching in her throat. 'He said to keep it safe. I understood nothing he tried to tell me about coding. But I think this box can help you. I think it talks to the quantum drive.'

Blake examined the box in his hands. It didn't look special in any way.

'We don't know how to use something like this,' Lola said, moving closer to Blake, her eyes on the box.

'I know someone,' Francesca said. 'She and Angelus were friends – they helped one another with coding and ... well ... things like that.'

'Who?' Blake asked eagerly.

'Her name's Sasha. She lives in Amber Zone – further south, close to the wall.'

'We have to find her,' Lola said, already getting ready to leave.

'Even EQ is crawling with Fr.e.dom soldiers now,' Blake said.

'But we have to find her,' Lola said. 'And find some way of letting androids know that those who uploaded are still alive. Imagine what that would do to Cardinal's control. It would be devastating.'

'How do we tell the androids of Lundun?' Blake asked.

Lola shrugged. 'Maybe this Sasha will know how.'

'She's not your normal android,' Francesca said.

Blake and Lola waited for more details.

'I've never spoken to her. She's shy – she doesn't go out or see anyone. I'm not even sure she will agree to speak to you.'

'She will,' Lola said. 'When we tell her what Angelus has done.'

Francesca bit her lip but said nothing.

Blake's instincts told him they should lie low and stay out of sight. But Lola was right – the androids needed to know the truth. And if there was some way of communicating with the quantum drive and the New Net, then they had to find it.

After convincing Francesca to allow Stig and Trevor to stay with her, Blake and Lola set off on bikes. The soldiers who had made it into Amber Zone were concentrating on the apartment towers, collecting the bodies of those who had uploaded. It would take them a long time to find all the bodies, which meant Blake and Lola could travel through the zone with little trouble. This freedom wouldn't last much longer; they had to make the most of it.

The co-ordinates Francesca had given him led to the oldest, most dilapidated apartment tower in the whole of EQ – maybe even in Lundun. Several huge digi-adverts rolled up, down and across the huge apartment towers, appealing to no one.

They pulled up outside the tower. The area was deserted. Anyone who lived here was certain to have uploaded.

Lola stared up at the tower. 'There's no way she's still in there.'

Blake checked the co-ordinates then walked through the front door. The lift looked like it had stopped working a long time ago, so he climbed the stairs. Graffiti unlike any he'd seen before covered the stairwell. The building was hellish, their steps echoing with an eerie emptiness. Along with the damp air in the stairwell, a rotten smell wafted through the building; Blake was almost ready to agree with Lola and go back.

They reached the forty-first floor. The whole tower was deathly quiet. Blake imagined android bodies in every room he passed, their consciousnesses with Angelus on the shuttle.

Part way down the hall, Blake found apartment thirteen. On the door was a sign. Its message was pretty straightforward: *Go away!*

After a quick glance at Lola, then along the hallway, he knocked.

No response.

He tried again.

Still nothing.

He tried shouting through the door. 'Sasha? I'm here

with Angelus.' It was a lie, but he figured he could explain if she answered.

Still nothing.

Lola took over the banging and shouting. She even tried to open the door, before taking out her pistol.

'No!' Blake said. He placed a hand on the door. 'Sasha, if you're in there, you have to let us in. We're coming in, anyway. There's a crazy woman right here with a pistol, ready to shoot down the door.'

He glanced at Lola and smiled.

'Crazy woman?' she whispered, frowning.

He shrugged.

He heard someone on the other side of the door.

'What do you want?' It was a feeble, mouse-like voice – not what he was expecting.

'We're here because of Angelus. We need your help.'

'Did you read the sign?' she asked.

'Yeah, I saw the sign. But we really need your help.'

'I can't help you.'

'We think you can. This is important. Angelus sent us.'

'He didn't send you here. He wouldn't.'

Lola took over again. 'Maybe not directly. But we need you to help us communicate with the quantum drive Angelus is keeping safe from Cardinal and Fr.e.dom.'

There was silence on the other side of the door.

Lola raised an eyebrow, ready to finish the job and get them inside. 'Angelus knows you're the only one who can help us.'

A moment later, there was a click and a bolt was slid back. Then the door opened. The voice Blake had heard through the door moments earlier did not match the person he saw.

# FORTY-FIVE

BLAKE WAS USED to meeting all kinds of androids. But even now, some of them surprised him.

'Have you stared for long enough?' Sasha asked, giving them room to enter her apartment.

But stare was all Blake – and Lola – could do. Many androids had seams on show – as a way of declaring they were android and proud of it. But Sasha had no seams, because she hardly had any skin at all, except for on one arm and her face. Her mane of pink hair was one of the few signs that she'd been built to look human at all. The rest of her body was the brushed silver of android alloy, apart from one tattooed arm and her legs, which were covered in long black mesh boots.

Finally, Lola walked into the apartment. Blake followed.

Sasha did not appear interested in explaining, so Blake didn't ask why she had no skin. But his eyes were fixed on her exoskeleton as she walked across the apartment. Some of the alloy had turned a coppery colour, and he saw the servos inside her joints whirring silently. It was a stark reminder of who he was, and yet to see her like that said nothing about how he felt about being android. He knew what he was seeing was true, that beneath his own skin, was the same exoskeleton. Still, it was unbelievable.

'I'm human,' Lola told Sasha.

Blake wasn't sure why she'd said it.

'I guessed,' Sasha said.

Her body, naked in a way that gave the word a new meaning, was right there before him, but he couldn't take his eyes off her face, part of it hidden by pink hair. She had the prettiest face he thought he'd ever seen. He couldn't take his eyes off her.

Lola stuttered, 'It's just, seeing you ... like that ... I felt I should tell you.'

Sasha nodded, unmoved.

Blake was still waiting for an explanation, but Sasha appeared impatient for *him* to explain why he and a human were threatening to shoot down her door.

He took the red box from his pocket and offered it to her. 'Angelus left this behind.'

'Left it behind? Where is he?'

In his stupor, Blake had forgotten to tell her what had happened. He cleared his throat and composed himself. 'Angelus and I took the data from Fr.e.dom's servers and saved it to a quantum drive. We saved most of the androids who had uploaded onto the Net.'

'You have a quantum drive?' she asked, and for the first time, looked eager to hear more. 'How? Angelus didn't make it. We couldn't do it.'

'Turing,' he said. 'The Messiah.'

Her upper lip curled.

'Do you know him?' he asked.

'I knew of him. Hell of a coder. But he's dead. I saw Cardinal kill him.'

'Cardinal wants the quantum drive and all the androids on it. He wants to punish those who have uploaded.'

'Where is the quantum drive?'

'That's the thing. The space shuttle that Fr.e.dom just launched – Angelus is on board, with the quantum drive.'

Sasha looked unmoved at first, but then her eyes sparkled pink, the same shade as her hair. 'Angelus is on a space shuttle?' She smiled a little. 'With a quantum drive?'

Blake pointed to the red box in her hand. 'And Angelus made that so we can communicate with him and the drive.'

She examined the red box, then glanced at Blake and Lola. 'What's a human doing in Lundun?'

'I want what he wants,' she said, nodding at Blake.

'And what's that?'

'For humans and androids to be free to live alongside one another.'

Sasha tilted her head, confused.

'Can you help us?' Blake asked. 'If we can contact Angelus then let androids know that those who uploaded are safe, it will undermine Fr.e.dom's control.'

'And what would that do?'

He wanted to tell her that it would make all the difference. But in truth, he didn't know if it would do anything in the long run. Even so, androids deserved to know.

'I don't know any more,' he said. 'Androids in Lundun appear to have given up. They're ready to do as they're told and fall in line. It's in their nature.'

Sasha took the red box to her terminal and sat down. 'In their nature? You mean, their programming?'

'Maybe.'

She placed the red box on the table and swiped the digi-screen on her terminal. 'Do you really believe that? That androids can't exert their own will, can't think for themselves?'

'I don't know.'

'Do you feel that way? Do you feel that you're following a program?'

He thought for a moment. 'No.'

'But you think other androids are different to you?'

'I'm not sure.'

'For an android who has risked a great deal, you don't seem too sure of much.'

He felt foolish, and annoyed.

'Can you help us or not?' Lola asked.

Sasha looked her up and down, then sneered. 'I will help Angelus. If I can.' She faced her terminal and set to work. Without turning, she pointed to a table beneath a window, laden with bottles of Grit. 'Help yourself.'

Blake grabbed a bottle, downed it, and handed another to Lola.

'I could do with one,' Sasha said.

Blake poured two more Grits and placed one on the table beside the red box. Sasha sipped the drink before glancing over to Lola, who had walked to the window to look outside.

'Tell me,' she whispered to Blake. 'Do you love her?'

It caught him off guard. 'What do you mean? I don't know what you're talking about.'

'I've never seen a human in love with an android before.'

He couldn't meet her eyes, but instead met Lola's, who stared at him intently. There was something different about her gaze – as if she was asking something of him.

'She's not—'

'For an android, you're pretty clueless.' Sasha tapped

then swiped the digi-screen. 'Angelus is really in space? In a shuttle?'

'Yes,' he said, wanting her to talk more about Lola, but unable to find a way to ask.

'He always was a crazy android. But if anyone can pull it off, Angelus can.'

Blake listened to her talk, but all he could think about was Lola and the stare she'd given him – a stare that, he realised, had been filled with jealousy.

# FORTY-SIX

BLAKE SAT NEXT to the window, gazing out onto Amber Zone. It was quiet, waiting for Fr.e.dom soldiers to arrive. The bodies of androids who had uploaded, now being dragged from their homes inside those apartment towers, reminded each and every android what might happen to them.

It had been three hours since Sasha had started trying to connect to the quantum drive on the shuttle. Blake wanted to understand what it would mean if they could contact Angelus and the quantum drive. He wanted everyone in Lundun to know that the androids were alive. Surely this would give them belief and undermine Fr.e.dom's control.

Lola sat opposite him and offered him a glass of Grit. He took it and swallowed a mouthful.

'I was ready to do it,' she said. 'I was ready to get on the shuttle.'

'I know.'

'Really. I was prepared. I want you to believe me when I tell you I see androids and humans as equals.'

'I believe you.'

She sighed heavily. 'I don't think you do. It's because I chose Jack, isn't it?'

He didn't know what to say.

'I knew there was a chance of bringing you back. But with Jack, I—'

'You don't have to explain.' No matter how often he tried to tell himself she had no choice, he couldn't shake the idea that it had been because Jack was human and he was android.

'I think I have something,' Sasha said.

Blake and Lola spun around in their seats, then got up to see.

Sasha spoke quickly. 'It uses quantum coupling. It's remarkable. I've never seen anything like it.' She stared up at the ceiling, as if the space shuttle, Angelus, and the quantum drive were on the other side. 'Angelus did it.' She laid a hand on the box. 'He created a bridge between here and the quantum drive, using quantum coupling.'

Blake stared at the terminal and the digi-screen, with no idea what the coding meant.

'What do we do now?' Lola asked.

'We enter the New Net ourselves and see if it works.'

Blake leaned closer to the digi-screen. 'We can go there?'

Sasha nodded.

'How?' Lola asked.

Sasha opened a drawer in her desk and took out a pot of Mirth pills. 'I hook you up and away you go.'

'So we can visit them?' Blake asked.

'More than that. It might be possible to upload permanently.'

Immediately, Blake saw the danger in this. How many androids would want to leave Lundun, the UK, or any other part of the world if they knew the New Net was a real alternative? But then, who was he to stand in anyone's way?

'I don't want you to go,' Lola said to him. 'We don't know if it will work. You might end up trapped there – or, worse, trapped somewhere else.'

Blake stared at the digi-screen. 'We need to know they're okay – that Angelus did it.'

Lola's shoulders drooped.

Sasha was preparing the connection, sorting through wires she could use to attach Blake to the terminal and the quantum drive.

'I don't like this,' Lola said.

Blake sat on a chair beside the terminal and let Sasha attach wires to his head and chest. She handed him the Sky-blue Mirth and he threw the pill into his mouth, swallowing it with a mouthful of Grit.

Lola had given in and sat beside him.

'It'll be okay,' he said. 'I'll check it has worked and the androids are alive, then I'll come straight back.'

Lola nodded. He imagined her kissing him, but instead, she stared at Sasha and the terminal, clearly apprehensive.

Sasha tapped the keys on her terminal and looked at Blake. 'Are you ready?'

He nodded.

She appeared worried. 'I'm not sure of the geography inside the New Net, so I've placed you where it looks like most of the activity is centred.'

He nodded again, but this time more uncertainty.

The Mirth was taking hold, working across his shoulders, making him shiver, then threading down his spine into the small of his back. The sensation rose up his neck and into the back of his head. It felt warm, almost euphoric: he felt himself slipping through the floor, through the earth, until he was weightless.

Then he was standing on the edge of the immense land mass floating in the sky he'd seen in the Net when he'd visited with Turing. It was the same world, but at night. The sky was a blanket of black, sparkling with stars. For all he knew, it might be the view of the universe outside the shuttle. He set off down the stone staircase towards the village below, its lights twinkling in the darkness. It had worked. Here was a complete digital world, outside Lundun – outside the world.

When he reached the bottom step, he saw someone waiting for him beneath a row of pergolas covered in pink flowers.

'Greetings, Postman,' a silhouetted figure said. Blake recognised the voice. It was Turing.

Blake walked closer until he could see Turing's face. He was smiling, his hands held out to embrace Blake. Blake let him, still unsure whether he could trust him.

'You did it,' Turing said, letting go.

'Has it worked?' Blake asked.

Turing turned towards the village, his arms outstretched. 'Yes. And it's all down to you.'

Blake walked through the row of pergolas and scanned the village. There were androids everywhere, dancing and singing.

'They owe it all to you,' Turing said. 'They have been reborn and are safe. Because of you.'

The sound of music drifted on the cool night air. At that moment, Blake felt the warmth of success – maybe they *had* done it.

'Follow me,' Turing said. 'I want you to meet someone.'

Blake followed him past more pergolas until they

reached the village itself. Entering a narrow street, they walked along a cobbled path until they arrived at a house. Turing knocked on the door. It swung open.

'Angelus?' Blake said, surprised.

'Blake!' Angelus walked out and embraced him.

'You did it!' Blake said. 'You uploaded.'

Letting him go, Angelus walked into the house. 'Come inside.'

Blake took one last look around the village, which was bursting with life and celebration, so different to Lundun, then followed Angelus and Turing inside.

# FORTY-SEVEN

BLAKE REMEMBERED, from his first visit to the New Net and Turing, how lemonade tasted. But the memory was nothing like the experience. Turing had used the same programming here, and Blake stared into the fizzy clear liquid, wondering how it was possible.

'Have you spoken to Francesca?' Angelus asked.

Blake offered a sympathetic smile. 'Yes. And now I can tell her it worked – that you're alive.' Using the word 'alive' had a new meaning now. Blake was still processing the idea. But Angelus *was* alive – he was right there, sitting on a chair, drinking lemonade.

Angelus gave Turing a fleeting glance. Blake felt he was missing something. 'What is it?' he asked.

Turing crossed his legs and leaned back in his chair. 'We must be careful.'

'How so?'

'We feel it's important to keep a certain amount of what we have done here secret.'

'Secret?'

'For now. Cardinal will know we have most likely been

successful. But he will not know that we have developed quantum coupling, allowing the transfer of consciousness. If he discovers this, he will try to use it against us. He can travel to the New Net digitally. Maybe even devise some kind of virus to infect the coding on the space shuttle.'

Blake waited for Angelus to explain further, but he was silent.

'They need to know,' Blake said. 'The androids of Lundun need to know that those they love are alive.'

Turing nodded sympathetically. 'They will. One day.'

'It would be wrong to keep this from them.'

'We have to,' Angelus said. 'For the sake of them all.'

'I don't understand.' Blake exhaled noisily. 'Why did we do what we did if we can't tell androids we won ... that we beat Cardinal?'

'It's not that simple,' Turing said. 'We can't let Cardinal discover how we're communicating.'

Blake sighed and stared at the floor. 'So what happens now?'

Turing uncrossed his legs and leaned forward. 'We're going to undermine Cardinal, one android at a time.'

Blake glanced at Angelus, who was clearly on board with Turing's plan.

'We will keep the quantum coupling to ourselves for now. If we share this ability, there will be many androids who wish to upload and come here. In time, that may be possible. But for now, we need to keep this from Cardinal.'

'So what do you want me to do?'

'We want you to send word to androids, one at a time, from those androids who are alive and well here.'

Blake shook his head slowly. 'One at a time?'

Turing nodded. 'Yes. You will be the medium through which androids here and in Lundun communicate.'

'But there are millions of androids here. I can't do that.'

'It will be slow work, and you won't reach all of them. But if you do this, then slowly androids will grow to believe that this place exists. That will undermine Cardinal's power and control.'

'I still don't see why I can't tell everyone at once. Surely that will give us more chance of undermining Fr.e.dom.'

'It is too dangerous,' Turing said. 'Besides, I believe doing it this way will have a longer-lasting, more powerful effect. Humans created androids to think and behave like them. Mythology, mystery and story have a powerful place in an android's mind, as they do in human minds. Imagine how this idea will grow in Lundun – even across the world. One by one, androids will hear from those they love and learn that this place exists. There will be a place for them to come when it is time. They will see all those they love again.'

'You're describing an afterlife.'

Turing smiled wryly, and Blake couldn't help feeling a little uncomfortable. There was something unsettling about the idea.

'Cardinal won't compete with this place. The Net he designs will be controlled, policed. But here, androids will be truly free. The story of this place will evolve and grow. Androids, like the humans who designed us, are drawn to stories. And there is no more powerful story than this. We must use it.'

Blake thought it through but, no matter how he viewed it, he came back to wanting to tell all the androids what they'd done.

'How do I do it?' he asked. 'How do I tell them?'

'You're a postman,' Angelus said. 'You take letters to androids.'

'Letters?'

'We can transcribe letters from androids, sharing information only they would know in order to prove they're still alive. You can deliver these letters.'

'But Cardinal has Lundun locked down. It won't be long before no one can move freely.'

Turing stood and walked to the window. 'It will be difficult at first. But this will grow. The letters will become a part of life in Lundun. It will work. I know it will.'

'He'll be looking for me. For Lola, too.'

'You have the spectrum,' Angelus said. 'Use it. You can stay ahead of Cardinal and Fr.e.dom. Stay in the shadows, delivering messages from those who live here to androids in Lundun.'

Blake considered what Angelus was saying. He still couldn't control the spectrum. It was more the other way around. The spectrum had a hold on him, surprising him and draining him of energy. It was more a destructive force than one he could bend to his will.

'You can do this,' Angelus said. 'And I have the first letter for you to write. For Francesca.'

Blake nodded, but he was in a daze, working through what they were asking him to do.

'We're playing a long game,' Angelus said. 'But in time, this will work.'

'I hope you're right.' Blake turned to Turing. 'Your friend you told me about, in Scotland – did you tell me the truth? Can he help me with the spectrum?'

Turing nodded. 'Malachi? Yes. Go to him. He will help you focus your mind and your ability.'

'It won't be easy,' Blake said. 'First, I have to escape Lundun, then head north through areas occupied by humans.'

Turing sat on the floor and crossed his legs. His back straight, he inhaled deeply.

Angelus took Blake outside. They stared up at the night sky and the stars. They looked different in a way Blake couldn't describe exactly. But it was as though he was taking in the night sky from a different world, a different part of the galaxy.

'Is there a waterfall here?' Blake asked, remembering what the android in River Zone, Kaz, had told him.

Angelus smiled. 'There are many.'

'Can I see one?'

He followed Angelus through a grove, tall trees in every direction. They walked along a woodland path, the green vegetation bursting with vitality. He ran his hands through the dense foliage of bushes that ran beside the path, moisture covering his skin.

As they walked, they reminisced about Lundun and how it looked at night, glowing with luminous reds and yellows and greens. Their descriptions were laced with nostalgia but Blake knew as well as Angelus, that Lundun was an unforgiving city.

They walked for some time, until they emerged from the trees and were confronted by a lake. It was the lake Kaz had described. Along the left hand side were rows of wooden cottages. And at the far end, was a tall, mountainous ridge, running through the centre of which was a waterfall. He focused on it and heard the distant crash of water.

He recalled Kaz lying beside her partner, dead. She couldn't take it any longer. Maybe she'd killed herself because she'd seen a place like this and knew deep down that she would never see it again. It was a painful thought.

'Can we get closer?' Blake asked.

They strolled along the right hand side of the lake. The

roar of the waterfall grew in volume as they got closer. Finally, Blake stood as close as he could. It was stunning. He gazed up at the water falling from such a great height. He followed it down to the lake, where the huge volume of falling water crashed at the bottom, sending plumes of water vapour into the air. On the other side of the waterfall, the sun was coming up. The warm sunlight was a dark yellow on the horizon, and through the mist of the waterfall, he saw the spectrum of light. But this wasn't the many worlds, this was in this reality, sunlight taken apart by droplets of water.

Angelus stood beside him. 'It's beautiful, isn't it?'

'Beautiful,' Blake agreed.

'They've given this place a name,' Angelus said.

'The New Net?'

Angelus nodded. 'I've heard them use it.'

'What is it?'

'The Garden.'

Blake considered the name, remembering another of William Blake's poems in the book he had been given – 'The Garden of Love'. It was unsettling to think how androids had adopted humanity's symbolism and desire for what felt like religious imagery. But maybe it didn't need to be like that. Maybe this digital home really could be a garden for androids.

'Thank you,' Blake said.

'What for?'

'For getting into the shuttle before Lola. It was brave of you.'

'Not really.' Angelus smiled. 'Besides, you can't shoot me here.'

Blake smiled back at him.

Angelus handed him a letter. 'For Francesca.'

Blake took it.

'I will take it to her,' Blake said, pushing the letter into his pocket. He turned again to the waterfall. 'It is miraculous.'

Angelus gazed at the waterfall too, but said nothing. No more words were needed.

# FORTY-EIGHT

BLAKE KNOCKED on the door and waited, Lola beside him. Someone was moving on the other side of the door, maybe looking through the spy hole. Chains, then locks were removed and the door opened a little.

'What do you want?' a woman asked through the narrow crack.

'I'm Blake,' he said. 'I have a letter for you.'

There was a frantic rattle. The door closed, then opened fully. A woman stood there, her arm outstretched, her eyes focused on the letter in Blake's hand.

'Is it … one of those letters?'

'There are no other letters,' Lola said, smiling.

The woman hesitated. Blake handed over the letter.

'It's true? They're still alive?'

'It's true,' Blake said.

The woman stepped out into the doorway, holding the letter close to her chest. She then put a finger to her lips. 'I have to keep it quiet, don't I? Gerry on the fourth floor got one. I heard. But you can trust me. I'll keep it to myself.'

Blake knew she wouldn't, but that was sort of the point.

He'd delivered enough letters now that the idea had spread throughout Lundun. People knew what these letters meant, even though Cardinal and Fr.e.dom still insisted they'd destroyed the quantum drive and had killed every android on it.

The woman had tears in her eyes. 'I loved her,' she said. 'Rachel. I really loved her. I couldn't believe it when I found out she'd uploaded. I wanted to tell her how much I loved her. But ... well ... I never could.'

'We'll leave you alone with the letter,' Blake said.

'Thank you, Postman.' The woman hesitated.

'What is it?' Blake asked.

She frowned. 'Where is she exactly?'

Blake thought for a moment. 'In the Garden.'

The woman appeared to be about to ask a question, but then her face changed and she smiled. 'I like that. The Garden. There are very few gardens here in Lundun.'

'Very few,' he said.

The woman nodded and closed her door.

Blake left her door and walked along the hallway with Lola.

'It must make you happy – getting to tell androids good news like that,' Lola said.

'It beats the deliveries I used to make.' Blake paused. He'd made some progress with controlling the spectrum. Now, it worked for him – telling him to take the stairs. 'There are soldiers in the lift,' he said, pulling Lola towards the door to the stairs.

She followed him and they descended the stairwell.

He'd grown accustomed to giving in to the sensation, and Lola had learned to trust him.

So many times he'd been close to asking her about their kiss outside the space shuttle. But things had changed since then. Lola had returned to focusing on the cause and the job in hand. There was no room for how he felt about her. It hurt, but at least he was close to her. Maybe that was all he needed.

They reached the ground floor and exited the tower into a dark and wet Lundun. EQ, like all other quadrants in Lundun, was again under Fr.e.dom's control. But if you knew which roads to take, which areas to stay clear of at what times, you could make your way around parts of Lundun.

He stood beside his bike.

'What's wrong?' Lola asked.

'I want to go to Scotland and find the android Turing told me about.'

'The android who sees the spectrum?'

He got onto his bike and started the solar-jet. It whispered with power. 'I need to know what I can do with it. I still don't have full control.'

Lola started her bike too. 'You seem to be doing fine.'

'I can take it so far. But I saw what Turing could do. If I can do the things he could, then there's a chance we might actually stop Fr.e.dom.'

Lola smirked.

'What?' he asked.

'Nothing.' She sat up straight on her bike. 'You've changed, that's all.'

'Changed?'

'Angelus always had faith in you. I thought he was crazy.'

Blake raised an eyebrow. 'Thanks.'

'How do we get to Scotland?'

'Do you think these bikes will get us through the tunnel one more time?'

Lola looked down at her bike. 'I'm willing to give it a go.'

He took in Lundun one last time: the sights, sounds and smells of home.

'Catch me if you can,' Lola said. She winked before vanishing, her solar-jet a flash of honey yellow powering her through Lundun at night.

He followed her and thought he would follow her anywhere she wanted to go, whether she asked him to or not.

The End of Book Two

# THANK YOU!

Thank you for being a reader and taking the time to read my book, the second in the Cyberpunk Uploads series.

I'm an indie writer of sci-fi: dystopian, post apocalyptic, and cyberpunk fiction. As I'm an indie, I am very much dependent on reviews. If you could spare the time, I'd be hugely grateful if you could leave an honest review of *Messiah Online* for me.

And please visit sethrain.com if you'd like to stay in touch. I'd love to hear from you.

For now, all the best.

Seth.

SETHRAIN.COM

Printed in Great Britain
by Amazon

54675526R00151